PEACE ON EARTH

PEACE ON EARTH

A Mystical Path to Free Agency

DR. KENNETH REX LARSEN

(Son of Israel, King of the Canaanites)

iUniverse, Inc.
Bloomington

Peace On Earth
A Mystical Path to Free Agency

iUniverse books may be ordered through booksellers or by contacting:

iUniverse
1663 Liberty Drive
Bloomington, IN 47403
www.iuniverse.com
1-800-Authors (1-800-288-4677)

ISBN: 978-1-4620-5903-4 (sc)
ISBN: 978-1-4620-5904-1 (e)
ISBN: 978-1-4620-5905-8 (dj)

Printed in the United States of America

iUniverse rev. date: 10/24/2011

Acknowledgments

I want to thank the following friends who reviewed my manuscript and gave useful suggestions: Paolo Barattini, Jim Cadman, Ben Valdez, Bryant Larsen, Scott Bergeson, David Reed, Bob Madrid, Steve Gustaveson (Hank), David Marsh, Bill Hinz.

Foreword

This little story is just a dream. Even if it does not reflect your exact reality, I hope it will still be relevant. This story is imaginary, based on my memory of existing stories and legends. Some of these ideas may be available to us from the same source. We work to inspire each other to grasp such concepts for ourselves.

Near the end of the 1982 movie *Gandhi*, Miriam, Gandhi's English disciple, tells an American reporter that Mahatma Gandhi knew the secret to peace. At the time I saw this movie, I thought she was referring to his nonviolent methods. But that was just his strategy for victory. Gandhi's greatest contribution, in my opinion, came after India's independence. The Muslims and Hindus were struggling for control of the country. The flagpole at Gandhi's residence bore no flag; he refused to take sides. The secret to peace is for government not to take sides in religious and cultural issues. Dr. Martin Luther King Jr. followed Gandhi, not only in nonviolence as a strategy, but also in his dream for a world of tolerance. He did not preach dominance of either race.

The daydream that is my book seeks to recapture the

spirit of the notable efforts of Gandhi and Dr. King in order to illustrate the advantages of a government's refusal to take sides. I expect that nearly everyone has taken a side in a religious or cultural issue, so you might be offended if I have not taken your side. If not, then either we are spiritual clones who agree on all issues, or you have reached a level of spiritual maturity beyond offense, and the world is blessed by your presence.

If you find something outrageous or offensive in this book, I suggest you consult your own inner source of truth—maybe with a quiet meditation in the mountains. If your truths are vindicated, they will be stronger, and you will expound on them with more power. If you are prompted to discover some previously unknown inner truth, this story can be a spiritual blessing.

I sincerely hope you will not accept my principles without checking your own inner source. Part of the mechanism of peace is to tolerate each other's beliefs. I only ask that you tolerate my personal beliefs, as herein presented, as you would want me to tolerate yours.

Ken Larsen
August 1, 2011

Chapter I

Santa's Little Gift

OUR STORY BEGINS ON Christmas Eve. I'm about to finish being Santa for one more year. I make a pretty good Santa. I put on his costume, and he speaks through me. I'm perfectly shaped to be Santa. I'm five feet nine inches tall and weigh about 230 pounds. The Santa outfit is snug but not tight. The beard and wig are perfect. Some women have even said I'm an attractive Santa.

I work as Santa at the Valley Fair Mall. I'm seated at the top of a double stairway so that my elves can lead the children up one side and go down the other. I think the decorations are older than I am—dusty snowflakes and snarls of white lights abound. Oblivious to the stale atmosphere, the children, in excitement or fear, come up and anxiously sit on my lap. Some kids are screaming; their parents try to pacify them in the face of this bearded stranger. The photographer only adds to the mayhem, but the store insists that he get each child on film for the parents. I don't care about the parents. I just want to give each child a magic moment. In the case of crying infants, I encourage the mother to sit on my lap, holding her child.

That usually works. Somewhere in the madness, I try to have a personal conversation with each child.

"*Ho-ho-ho!* Merry Christmas, Martha. You remember what I said—do what your mommy says and have a very happy Christmas this year."

"Thank you, Santa," says a cute little four-year-old as she scampers triumphantly from her experience on my lap.

"*Ho-ho-ho!* And here comes my last little visitor. Well, actually, you're not so little, are you? So, climb up here on my knee and tell me your name."

"My name is Billy. Billy Mitchell," he says as he straddles one knee. "And you would know it if you were the real Santa Claus."

It looks like Billy is about nine or ten, but his furrowed brow and intense concentration depict a boy wiser than his years. His suspicious commentary suggests he isn't the little boy I would have expected. Oh, well, I'm Santa to the end. It's time again to pull out my Santa channeling trick.

"Well, Billy, I am the real Santa Claus. Right now, I'm renting this body from a mortal just like you. His name is Ken Larsen. He lets me use his body every year so that I can talk to all my friends, like you."

"Wait a minute," says Billy with a judgmental scowl. "You're talking about yourself as if you were someone else. I'm too smart for that kind of nonsense."

"It's called channeling," Santa explains with my voice. "Ken puts on my outfit and channels me. Oh, don't be so negative. We're all born with it. Sometimes it's called having an imaginary friend, like you did a few years ago. All children are born with special abilities. They naturally know how to dance, sing, laugh, love, and channel. Usually, they think they have to lose these things to grow up. They learn how to sit still when they feel like dancing or singing. They learn how to hate others for being different. They learn that imaginary friends aren't politically correct. Then, later, they learn again how to sing and dance. Ken was one of the lucky ones who learned again how to channel. Once you get the hang of it, you can channel anyone or anything, dead or alive, real or imaginary. When children channel, it's called having an imaginary friend. When adults do it, they are called mediums or prophets. Ken channels me, and you get to talk to Santa. It's that simple."

Judging from his displeased expression, Billy's suspicion is deepening. With a scowl, he says accusingly, "Sounds to me like you need help."

"I'm sure I do, Billy," I admit. "We all need help. That's why we are all here—to help and to be helped. Actually, I think the sick ones are those who hide their different personalities from each other, or even worse, those who deny their natural channeling to avoid ridicule."

"I think it's all in your imagination," says Billy.

"Of course it is," I respond. "Everything is imaginary. That's why it's fun and harmless. Anyway, Ken's body and his mind are all I've got. He has stuffed his little brain with all kinds of nonsense, like science, history, and politics. There just isn't room for all the names of the six billion children on the earth."

"Isn't that the whole population?"

"Yes, Billy. My, you're very smart for a ten-year-old boy. Yes, that's the whole population of the world, and Santa sees a child in the heart of each one."

"How did you know my age?"

"Oh, just a good guess, I guess."

"You're different from the other Santas."

"How's that?"

"You're honest ... crazy, but honest."

"Thank you, Billy."

"The others pretend their fake beard is real," Billy says, as the concerned furrows on his forehead smooth out and he scoots a little closer. "They encourage the other kids to believe in something that can't be real." Billy surprises me with a friendly yank on my beard. "Oh!" he cries. "Your beard doesn't come loose."

"No," I explain, "it's securely tied with a shoelace on the back of my head. You want to hear a funny story? A few years ago, I grew my own beard. It was several inches long, but it wasn't white, so I wore the Santa beard over it. Some kids asked about my beard, and I pulled off the Santa beard, revealing my own beard underneath. Boy, then they knew I was the real Santa for sure."

Billy laughs out loud. "Those other kids sure were stupid to believe Santa is real just because you grew a beard."

"Oh, Billy, don't be so sure. Santa may not be a physical person. But that doesn't mean he isn't real. Santa is also a feeling. He's that feeling of joy you get when you give to another. He's that joy you feel when you do something wonderful and nobody knows, not even your mom. The joy is real, and you can feel Santa in your heart just by following his example and giving to others. And if, like me, you put on his costume, you just might channel that feeling into your own imaginary person. Oh, yes, Santa doesn't need a Social Security number to be real."

"Thank you, Santa. That's a good way to think about it."

The store manager interrupts. "Okay, Santa, we're running a bit late. Give the boy his candy cane and let's go. We've got our own families to get home to, and we don't pay overtime."

"Just another moment, please, Mr. Burton. Billy here hasn't yet made his request. And you can take my paycheck and give it to your favorite charity. Merry Christmas."

Mr. Burton steps down in a huff and dismisses the rest of my staff, leaving me alone with Billy. I think how much I'm going to miss that check. I ignore my financial needs as Ken and return as Santa to Billy.

"Now, Billy, where were we? Oh yeah, let's play a little game. You pretend just for a minute that I'm the real Santa Claus and that I can give you anything you want in the whole world, as long as it does not violate my rules of morality. What would you ask for?"

"Peace on Earth," he says with a mischievous gleam in his eye.

"Wow! You don't mess around, do you? I cannot grant that wish. Let me explain my rules a bit. Yes, I have my own prime directives. First of all, I do no harm. So, you can't ask me to punish your enemies or kill your neighbor's dog. Second, I do not force human behavior. I won't force other people to be peaceful."

"Why not?"

"Well, Billy, you see, if I forced people to do good, they would lose the joy of choosing right. Let's see ... let me put it this way. Do you remember when you were trying to learn to play the piano?"

"Yes, how did you know?"

"Just a good guess. Anyway, you made lots of mistakes and your music sounded terrible."

"Sounds like you were there," he says with embarrassment.

"Now, Billy, suppose your mother had sat down next to you and played all the notes for you. The music would have been beautiful, but you would not have learned to play."

"Yeah, she does play pretty good. Do you think her music was as bad as mine when she started?"

"Yes, Billy. That's how we learn—by making mistakes. Oh, I might be able to force everyone to be good, but then nobody would learn how to live. Here's another example: remember last Halloween when you stole some of Sally's candy? Nobody caught you and nobody punished you, but when you saw her cry you felt very bad. You learned two beautiful lessons. First, you learned how much you really love Sally. Then, you learned that you feel bad when you hurt someone you love. You couldn't learn those important lessons in living if someone always forced you to be good."

"Wow, Santa! You're right. It does hurt when I do bad," Billy said with enthusiasm. Then the suspicion returned to his face. "How did you know I stole the Halloween candy, and how did you know Sally's name?"

"Just another lucky guess. Don't worry, Billy. Your secret is safe with Santa. That's another one of my rules. I keep your secrets because I respect your free agency."

"Free agency?" asks Billy.

"Yes, free agency—the right to make your own choices," I respond. "Even when you are hurting others, I respect your free agency for two very important reasons. First, if I forced you to choose what I think is right, I would be stealing from you the blessings of choosing good by yourself. Second, only when I allow your free agency do I have a right to demand that you allow mine."

"Goodness!" says Billy. "This is really big. So, you are saying when I force others, I give them permission to force me. Is it the same as when I hit someone? That gives them permission to hit me?"

"Yes, exactly," I say. "That's a secret to life. You can't be free if you don't let others be free. Now, your mother has waited long enough. You are free to take these five candy canes home and give them to Sally. Tell her you took her Halloween candy and that you're sorry. Then, you will discover how wonderful you feel when you do good to someone. In fact, Billy, you feel even more wonderful if they don't deserve it. That's right. If you can love someone and do good for them even when they are hurting you, you will have special power. I'm not saying to let people hurt you. I'm saying to love them even when they hurt you. Then you will see how good you feel when you do. Don't love your enemies because you fear God. Love your enemies because it is a secret path to personal power and happiness. And Billy, it's even better if they don't know it's you. That's why people use Santa's name when giving Christmas presents."

Billy ponders silently while stroking his lips.

Suddenly, I scream through Santa's voice, "Oh my, Billy! Look at the time. I've got to go. I need to return this body to Ken so he can go visit his girlfriend. And I've still got to hear what he wants for Christmas!"

Billy pockets his candy, but his smile looks suspicious.

Without pondering his motives, I continue, "Oh yes, and one more thing, Billy. You did ask for peace on Earth, didn't you?

Well, here's a secret for peace within your own personal world. Just make sure, from now on, that everything you say and do is perfectly in agreement with what you really believe. That will put peace in your heart. And, as far as peace on Earth goes, here is a magical candy cane of peace." Billy's eyes sparkle with curiosity as he accepts the special confection. "Keep it separate from the others you are going to give Sally. When you get home, break this candy cane into two pieces. Take one piece outside and place it on the ground. Then, you will have your piece on Earth. *Ho-ho-ho!* Merry Christmas, Billy," I say as a Santa who can't help closing with a pun. "You've been wonderful, and I've got to run."

"Bye, Santa," says Billy with a laugh at my silly joke after such a serious discussion for such a youngster. As he leaves, I sense a sinister motive behind his suspicious smile.

Chapter II

Santa's Big Gift

THE RED BAG OVER my shoulder is full of presents for my girlfriend, Sandy. She's a beauty. I don't know what she sees in a fifty-eight-year-old, portly Santa wannabe. She lives on the top floor of a very old apartment building. I hear Santa's bells jingling as I trod up the six flights of stairs. *Ding-dong.* I ring her doorbell while catching my breath. She opens the door, and I'm reminded again how beautiful she is. Her flowing blonde hair is over her shoulders, and she has a body that makes any man happy to see her. I drop my bag as she showers me with hugs and kisses. She objects to the Santa beard, but I want to give her my presents while I'm still Santa. I bring my mind back from my hopes for a reward in the bedroom as we sit on the couch to exchange gifts. She's crazy about jewelry, so my first gift is a diamond bracelet. Although it is relatively cheap from the mall department store, it still took me six months to save up the cash. Sandy makes a bigger fuss than the gift is worth, probably to encourage future giving.

Sandy hands me a small box. It's obviously from that Egyptian shop in the mall. I open it to reveal a golden cartouche—an oval medallion imprinted with hieroglyphs. It's about an inch wide and two inches long. It is attached to a beautiful gold chain. Sandy is so excited to explain it to me. "It's your name!" she exclaims. "See? Kenneth Rex Larsen. The Egyptology lady was happy to explain your name to me. Here are my notes. K is a flat bowl with a ring handle. I think in ancient Egypt, it was an oil lamp, meaning that you bring light. For me, it's Santa's bowl full of jelly with those cute love handles." She tickles my love handle and gets a chuckle out of me. I tuck my shirt back in under my Santa suit as she smiles.

"Okay, okay," I laugh. "I prefer to bring light. I'm sure there are others with a K who don't have so much jelly. *Ho-ho-ho!*"

Sandy gets more serious. "The next letter was probably pronounced as A and is represented by an eagle. In my mind, it means you fly higher than any other bird. In the Egyptian language, the short E sound is automatically inserted between adjacent consonants, and it is probably the correct sound before the TH. The letter N is represented in two ways: the wavy line, signifying water or expanse, and the red crown of the north. I think it means you rule over many waters. Finally, the TH is a pair of fire tongs and means possession. You own something. You own Kenn. But if you put an extra E sound between the N's, like the Egyptians would, and pronounce the first E like an A, you get Kanen, or the land of Canaan. That's right. In Egyptian, your first name means 'owner or inhabitant of Canaan,' 'Canaaneth,' or 'Canaanite.'"

"So, I'm from Canaan, am I?"

"I'm sure you have ancestors who were, don't you?"

"No doubt. I suspect that of just about every European."

Sandy sounds like she's reading from an encyclopedia, "Your middle name, Rex, is a Latinized version of Ra, the sun god, so they inscribed your cartouche with Ra holding the scepter of authority and wearing the sun disk and the sacred cobra on his head. It means you bless others with your bright wisdom, and you rule like the mighty cobra. It also means you bring together the round yin and the straight yang."

"Right, and I'm sure you got all this from the store clerk," I say with a laugh as I brush a wisp of hair from her forehead.

"Shush. I'm telling it my way. I've been studying this stuff for a week, so you better believe me. Your last name is really fun. Rather than translate the letters directly into Egyptian, the store lady said that in Norwegian, Larsen means 'the son of Lars.' In Egyptian, to be the son of, or born of, is symbolized by those three lines that come together, like the end of the devil's pitchfork. It's pronounced *mes*, and it's part of the 'ms' in Ramses, meaning the son of Ra. The 'mos' in Moses represents the son of the nameless god."

"'Lars' was very interesting. Look, if you read it backwards, it's S–Ra–L, obviously intended by your Norwegian ancestors as code for Israel. The S is a bar with two little vertical lines in the middle, representing a bolt or fastener."

Now, she acts the part of a professor lecturing to her associate professor.

"Your name is completed with the god Ra, and a lion for the sound 'el.' I think it means something like the lion rules the earth, the sun god rules the sky, and the bolt fastens them into one. As you may know, the lion can represent either the R or L sounds." Her words tumble out faster, gaining speed, and I can't help but smile at her enthusiasm as she continues. "Maybe they are the female and male powers that the god Ra unites with his magic bolt. I went to the Bible and found that Jacob received the name Israel because he was like a prince with power over God and men, and he had prevailed. So, Dr. Larsen, you are the son of Israel, the uniter and controller of Earth and sky, or physical and spiritual. You are Rex or Ra, the ultimate ruler. Oh, Ken, I'm so intrigued by the symbolism in your name. It means you are a son of Israel and the king or leader of those who own or inhabit the land of Canaan." Triumphantly, she puts down her notes.

"You know, Sandy, my father's name was Rex—which you've said means Ra, or the god of all—and my mother's name was Mary, the same as the mother of Jesus. Also, I was born at the spring equinox, March 20, the same as Jesus, according to some traditions. Add that to your mystical symbolism," I say with a belly laugh.

"Don't laugh too hard, Ken," says Sandy with a judgmental look on her face. She picks up her papers and straightens them. "I think some of this stuff has meaning. According to your name, the land of Canaan is yours. Have you checked into it lately?" She smiles as if it were true. Expanding on her interpretation, she says, "Your property is in a mess. Jews and Muslims are killing each other almost every day. If you could, you should take charge and bring peace to the Holy Mount. Too bad it's just a dream." She smiles.

"Wow, Sandy, there's really a lot of interesting meaning in my name, isn't there? Why don't we hurry right over to Israel and assume my throne? I'm sure they won't mind giving me back my kingdom. I don't see why they should even require an election. Heh-heh. And I'll just raise my royal finger and everyone will be good."

"Well, Ken, I don't care what others think. Your name is special to me, and I kinda like being the king's girlfriend—King Santa." She bows gracefully, gently lifts my Santa beard, and attaches the gold chain around my neck. She kisses her king, definitely ringing Santa's bells. Of course, I'm thinking of her ringing my bells.

"Wow, Sandy, now I've got a gold dog tag. I missed being in the military. I didn't think I would ever wear a dog tag."

"Very funny. I'm sure that's the world's most expensive dog tag," she says with a playful push as she tucks the cartouche under my shirt.

"Wouldn't it be great, Sandy, if it were true? Wouldn't it be great if I could do something about that mess in Palestine today? Ya know, darling, I wish I could go to Israel and be well received. I wish I could go there and help those people find peace. I wish this was more than just an idle Christmas wish. Well, let's see what else Santa has for you in his bag. *Ho-ho-ho!*"

Ding-dong. The doorbell rings.

Sandy peeps through her peephole. "Oh, no!" she whispers. "It's Jed. I didn't think he would be coming tonight. I guess he thought I'd talk to him on Christmas Eve. Now what am I going to do?"

"Is anything wrong? Who's Jed?"

"Everything's wrong. He's my husband."

"*What?* You didn't tell me you were married."

"Only according to the law. We've been separated long enough. I was waiting for the right time to tell you. I was afraid

I might lose you. But now we've got a different problem. Jed's the jealous type, and he can't find you here. I'll tell you more later. Now you've got to hide on the fire escape. Here, take all this stuff."

Nervously, I climb through the third-story window onto the dilapidated metal platform. I gather my bag and other stuff in my left hand as I grip the icy railing with my right. I manage to keep Santa's bells from ringing while I wait for Sandy to get rid of Jed. I can hear them talking. Jed shouts at Sandy. Unconsciously, I grab my mouth. The worst happens. I slip on the ice, fall to the grate, and slide off into the air. The beauty of the icicles on the building nearly escapes me as I hear within me the words, "Oh, shit!"

Chapter III

Knock, Knock—Who's There?

I'M NOT DEAD. OR AM I? Looking down from a few feet above, I can see my body on the pavement. Blood slowly oozes from my face, making Santa's beard match the rest of his outfit. My right arm is folded strangely. I'm sure someone heard the crash and help is on the way. But somehow I'm not concerned with my body anymore. I look up at the night sky, and one of the stars seems very bright. It grows in brightness until it fills the sky. I guess I'm about to see for myself what an out-of-body experience is all about. I wait a while, but nothing happens. I continue to wait, but still nothing but stillness and whiteness. "Hey! Where is everybody?"

Silence.

"Aren't I supposed to be greeted by a guide or see my life or something?"

The stillness continues.

"Listen, I've got lots of dead people who really love me, and they're not going to like it if you keep me waiting like this. Is this all there is? I just sit here in all this white light while my body grows cold? Don't I get any information? Who's in charge here?"

"What do you expect?" says a voice in the whiteness.

"What do you mean, what do I expect? I expect to be greeted and shown around or something. After all, I'm the king of Israel."

"What I mean is, what do you expect? In this realm, you get what you expect. You haven't given us any expectation on which to build. How can we show you what you want to see if you don't want anything?"

"I want to see the truth."

"Which truth?"

"The truth."

"There are many truths, and you don't seem to be holding any of them. You don't even hold the absence of truth as your truth."

"Do I have to believe something before it can be true?" I ask.

"Yes," says the voice.

"What about science?"

"What about it? Science has no truths, only probabilities. Your scientist, Mr. Heisenberg, demonstrated that concept a hundred years ago with his uncertainty principle."

"What lies beyond my beliefs?"

"Nothing you could ever comprehend or understand; nothing that can be communicated in words, thoughts, visions, emotions, or any other code suitable for your mind."

"What about Jesus Christ?"

"Hello, Ken."

I see a man in a long white robe. He looks just like the

pictures of Jesus from Sunday School, except his hair and beard are white, like Santa's.

"Jesus, is that you?"

"Yes, Ken. I'm exactly as you imagine me to be."

"What about the other deities of mankind? What about Allah, the Buddha, the spirit of the Tao, Krishna, Elohim, Jehovah, voodoo, Thor, Mars, and Ra, the God whose name I have?"

"Which of them would you like to meet?"

"Which of them is true?"

"True for you?"

"No, true for the entire universe. I want to talk with the God of reality.

Jesus disappears. I hear nothing and see nothing. I feel apprehensive. "Hey," I shout, "please come back. I'm sorry. What did I say wrong?"

"Hi, Ken. It's Jesus again. Did you enjoy your conversation with the God of reality?"

"I didn't hear or see anything."

"Exactly."

"Okay, if you're telling me that all the gods I ever heard of are figments of the imagination, then what good are they?"

"Plenty. It is important that truth be allowed into the minds of men. Men need some kind of authority for that truth. Their gods give them that authority so that they can act and feel according to their truths. Without a god to tell them so, men might not realize the beauties of love, kindness, charity, mercy, and brotherhood. Without the authority of a god, they might not learn to avoid the pitfalls of hate, fear, revenge, and ego. They might never learn that it is better to win when there is no loser. They might miss the point that they are all parts of a single whole. Before they can enjoy the benefits of such true feelings and actions, they need a source. We give them the source they imagine."

"Are you going to send me back so I can tell others that there is no God?"

"No. You cannot tell them any such thing."

"Why not?"

"Because this conversation is a figment of your imagination."

"Wait a minute," I respond. "Does that mean your claim that the gods of others are figments of their imagination is merely a figment of my own imagination?"

"Yes."

"I am going back, am I not?"

"Yes."

"There was a reason for my being here, wasn't there?"

"Your question implies that some higher authority provides reasons. Have you decided which higher authority you want to see?"

"You mean which imaginary God I want?"

"Yes."

"No."

"Okay, Ken, here are the ground rules. You are here because Santa heard your Christmas wish. You will return to your body and you will have *the power*. With it, you will heal your own body and the bodies of others."

I sense a strong feeling of urgency in Jesus's voice. "Right now, your world is in chaos over power and religion. The center of that conflict is in Palestine, where Christians, Jews, and

Muslims are grappling over politics, power, and control of the world's resources. Each faith considers itself the rightful owner of land and wealth, and they're so willing to kill and be killed for their cause that they don't even realize how unnecessary it is. There is a way to peace. Your mission will be to go to Israel and help the world make peace. Through you, we are going to grant Billy's wish. You will be limited only by Santa's rules. Do you have any requests before you go?"

"Yes. First, could you please give me the wisdom of Solomon to go with all that power and to help me keep my ego under control?"

"Done. Solomon you shall be."

"Thank you. Second, could I please meet all the gods of mankind?"

"Yes, as many as possible within the time available."

Suddenly, I am in a giant open hall full of gods. The ceiling is so high I can hear an echo. One by one, the gods introduce themselves and hug me. As they do so, I feel them joining me and adding to my spirit. "Hello again, Jesus. Hi, Krishna." As I hug each God, I feel their distinct personalities. Some are firm and almost military, while others are more relaxed—it's like hugging my grandmother. Each is unique, yet all are the same. I feel the same unconditional love in every hug. "Hi, Buddha, Lao Tse, Santa Claus, Joseph Smith, Black Elk, Mars, Venus, Easter Bunny, Thor." As I hug and exchange love with each god, I hear the others talking among themselves. It's like a giant celestial cocktail party. The conversations are lively and often punctuated with loud laughter. I'm reminded of a reception line at a joyous wedding—my wedding, my marriage to the many forms of the one God. "Greetings, Odin, Ra, Jehovah, Lucifer,

Elohim (Ha-Shem), the many gods of voodoo, Moses, Zoroaster, Elijah." All assure me that they will be available to talk through me whenever I ask. I feel the legends of the centuries passing through my subconscious as I encounter all the gods of history. I realize that all their stories are suddenly available to my mind, as if each were putting a special book on a library shelf in my mind.

"Nice to meet you, Eastre, Baal, Tooth Fairy, Saturn, Mercury, Neptune, Allah, God the Father, Mother, Son, Daughter, Brother, Sister, Husband, Wife." I feel so full; I feel stuffed to the bursting point with spirituality. It's almost too much to bear. Oh, my head is swimming. So many gods. So many friends. So many stories. So much truth. So much pain—pain in my head, pain in my arm, pain in my back, pain in my legs, pain, pain, pain—just swimming in pain.

Chapter IV

A Painful Awakening

"It hurts."

"There, there, Santa. You're going to be all right. Somebody call Dr. Teasdale. He's coming around."

"Oooohhh."

"Hello? Is that you, Santa? Have you finally decided to come back?"

"Where am I?" I open my eyes and look around. My broken right arm is in a cast. I cannot feel my legs. My head is in a cement mixer. I'm surrounded by machines. Each of them has tubes or wires leading to my body. Most of the machines have TV screens with flashing lights. Some make little beeping sounds. In front of me is a very official-looking man in a white doctor's coat. He looks about my age, but he is much thinner. He has long, straight hair down the back of his head and is wearing black-rimmed glasses. In spite of his formal attire, he looks friendly.

After listening to my heart and lungs, he speaks. "You're in the University of Utah hospital intensive care unit. You've been unconscious for a week. Tonight is New Year's Eve. My name is Dr. James N. Teasdale. I'm from Chicago and somewhat of an expert on miraculous healings. Your Dr. Jones is a longtime friend of mine. He invited me to come and investigate the Santa who refuses to die."

Thinking about my brother who lives in Chicago, I absently mumble, "Wow, I've been hugging gods for a week!"

"What?" asks Dr. Teasdale, turning a knob on his recorder.

"Oh, nothing. So, I should be dead, should I?"

"Oh, yes. The injury to your head was more than sufficient to kill you. The details of your miraculous recovery have been in all the Utah papers. Everyone was afraid Santa had taken his last sleigh ride," he says with a grin as his hand portrays Santa flying.

"I thought you only teased Dale, Dr. Teasdale," I objected. "That's false advertising!"

Dr. Teasdale's eyebrows rise as he scribbles on his chart. "Everyone was worried about your mind. They've been working very hard to drain the fluid from your cranium. I'm thrilled to note that you are conscious and lucid enough to crack a silly joke. Tell me what you remember about your accident, including that remark about hugging Gods."

"I was with my girlfriend, Sandy, and her ex-husband came to the door. She asked me to hide on the fire escape. I slipped and slid off the platform into three floors of space. I noticed the icicles on the side of the building and then you."

"Anything between the icicles and me?"

"Well, yes, sort of."

"Meaning?"

"Well, I think I had an out-of-body experience."

Teasdale's face suddenly lights up with interest as he leans forward, holding up his hand recorder. "What do you remember of it?" he asks eagerly.

"I think I remember it all. It was very strange. I heard a voice. I met Jesus. In fact, I met every god I've ever heard about and some I hadn't. I was told that I would somehow heal my body and use my powers to bring peace to the world." I recite the rest of my out-of-body experience for Teasdale's recorder. I am surprised at the level of his interest.

Teasdale asks, "You're a scientist, aren't you?"

"Yes. I graduated from a PhD in lizards to a research associate professor of medicine. I do medical research right here in this hospital."

"Do you believe in God?"

"I used to be extremely devout and believing. But my science has confused me. I'm not so sure just who or what God might be, especially after my experience. In fact, I have a lot more questions than answers. How about you?"

"I'm a devout atheist," says Teasdale, puffing out his chest proudly, as if it were an accomplishment, "but I've seen plenty of strange and improbable medical healings. I believe we have mental powers far beyond those we understand. That doesn't mean there has to be some supernatural being out there controlling everything. I'm sure there's no such entity. I see no reason to invent some God just so we won't have to admit we don't know."

"So," I reply, "you don't explain things without God. You just deny God and leave things unexplained."

"Yes," Teasdale says, raising his voice in his excitement that I'm apparently getting it.

"That sounds sort of like some of the stuff I heard while out of my body," I say.

"Yes," says Teasdale, "doesn't it? Well, your case is rather unique. That's why I'm so excited to be here. I have written several books on phenomenal medical healings. I heard about your case and flew here from Chicago to personally monitor your healing. This is great. You should have been killed by the fall, but somehow you miraculously cheated death. There is no medical reason for you to have come out of your coma. And if you did wake up, you should have been very confused, like a drunk man. Yet you appear lucid. And now, you say you think you were given special powers by some spirit to heal yourself. Oh, Dr. Larsen, you are going to make a wonderful chapter in my book, maybe a whole book. We'll have a press conference tomorrow, and you will be a famous miracle."

"I'm sorry, Dr. Teasdale, we can't do that. I feel that I must keep my powers a secret until I can go to Israel and make peace."

"Just how many years do you expect me to keep you under wraps?" Teasdale says sternly.

"No, I get the notion that I'm going to do it this year, during the days of the Passover," I say, without understanding why.

"Obviously, you haven't heard the news. President Clinton is trying and failing to help the Israelis and Palestinians make peace. As always, the Israelis are continuing in their fight to rebuild their temple and their society, while the Palestinians just want their home back. There is talk of some kind of general revolt to coincide with Passover. Pilgrims and tourists are canceling their visits to the Holy Land for this year. Military security is getting very tight. The United States is sending warships to the eastern Mediterranean. It could be bigger than Desert Storm. It looks like we are joining with Europe on the side of Israel, while most of the Muslim world is falling in line with Palestine. I don't think you're going to Israel this year. Besides, you are in no condition to get out of this bed, much less travel across the globe. You focus on getting better and being my star miracle."

"No, Doctor, you must keep my powers a secret," I insist.

"Even if I wanted to, it will be almost impossible," says Teasdale, slapping the bed rail with his clipboard for emphasis.

Changing the subject, I ask, "Tell me what has happened while I've been gone."

"You mean besides the international news?"

"I mean in my life—the life that I apparently haven't been participating in for a while. Do my children know? What about my job and my apartment?"

"Well, everyone here at the hospital—including your supervisor—obviously is very understanding of your condition—"

"No, I mean my other job. Did somebody get my Santa suit to the cleaners? Because my supervisor is the grumpiest fifty-year-old elf you've ever—"

"Easy, easy—relax. Everything is under control. The important thing is that you are awake, and I will make you famous."

"Do you think we can keep my powers from the eyes of the media for three months?"

"I don't see how, but if you have the powers you claim to have, maybe it can be done. Why don't you rest a while? I promise not to tell anyone without your permission, at least until we can talk some more. And don't worry. I'll get Dr. Jones, your neurosurgeon, to issue a gag order for his staff."

With my left arm, I manage to eat some soup and crackers. I notice that hospital food hasn't improved since the last time I was here. I turn on the television and watch the ten o'clock news. I see that the doctor was right about Israel. If ever they needed a miracle it's now. I wonder how I'm going to do any good in my condition. I wonder how I'm supposed to heal myself in time to do any good. I like my attractive nurse, Suzy. I ask her about Dr. Teasdale.

"Oh, he's an odd one," she explains. "His training is in psychology and hypnotherapy. Some consider him a quack. He says he's an atheist, but he's documented some astonishing medical miracles. I'm not sure I believe some of his crazy stories." Suzy leans in a bit closer to whisper, "Dr. Jones, your neurosurgeon, has been a longtime friend and admirer of Dr. Teasdale. He has given Teasdale carte blanche to the place. I think he's beyond strange. He's downright weird. He has taken all kinds of sound and video recordings. He has convinced Dr. Jones to gather medical data on you that might not normally be required. He has interviewed at length nearly everyone who has come to visit. It concerns me that people come to see you, and they spend all their time talking to this hypno-psycho-babble weirdo. Speak of the devil—here he comes."

Chapter V

Getting Better

"Hı, Ken. I see you're talking to the nurse when you should be resting," says Teasdale, the tone of his voice suggesting that he somehow has exclusive rights to me. I suspect he and Suzy have had words.

"I *am* resting," I answer, raising my good arm in protest. "So, Doctor, you're researching miraculous healings, and yet you're an atheist? Why? Are you trying to prove there is no God by explaining away medical miracles? Do you intend to use me?"

"No. I intend to work with you. I accept medical miracles. I'm cataloging medical miracles to support my premise that it does not matter which God you believe; just as it doesn't matter which fantasy you use to enhance sex."

"Wait a minute," I interrupt. "Do you really believe that gods are no more than sexual fantasies? Now that's an interesting aspect of atheism."

"Yes, Ken, I expect to show that true believers in all religions can have miraculous healings and that whatever mechanism is involved, it has nothing to do with any particular theology.

27

As a scientist, you know you can't prove there is no God. But I believe my books present data that show that the name and characteristics of one's God are irrelevant. That's the second best thing to proving the nonexistence of any particular God. Yes, Ken, there are medical miracles. No, we don't understand them. And no, that doesn't mean there has to be some God out there. I intend to prove that miracles don't depend on some particular God or idea any more than good sex depends on imaginary fantasies."

"Fascinating. And you hope to use me to support your thesis?"

"Why not? You had what should have been a fatal fall. Then you recovered, and now you appear completely lucid. You claim you were given some special power by some unknown spirit or spirits. And to top it all off, you claim to have met all the gods, and they are apparently equal in your mind. You're the first subject I've studied who seems not to be relying on borrowed theology. Apparently, you don't have a theology, not even atheism, like me. You're the perfect subject for my next book. You don't have a problem with that, do you?"

"Not as long as you agree to postpone your story until I go to Israel," I say.

"So, you still think you're off to Israel, do you? Have you noticed your body?" Yes, but I was hoping he hadn't. "You have several serious skull fractures, a compound fracture of both the bones in your right forearm, several shattered vertebrae, and both your legs and ankles are badly broken. You expect me to keep quiet about you until you can go to Israel? That could be years," he objects.

"No, I expect you to keep quiet until the full moon on

April 8, the first day of the Jewish Passover, when I will be doing something in Israel."

"I can try to keep quiet, but if you heal yourself in time to be in Israel for Easter, it's going to be impossible to keep you out of the news." His concern is emphasized by pressing his clipboard against his stomach.

"You do your part, and my power will take care of the rest."

"You really believe you have some superhuman power, don't you?"

"Yes."

"Well, I'm okay with that. This conversation is good evidence that you have more than ordinary abilities. Maybe you are to spiritual power what Mozart was to music. So, do you want to start healing yourself now, while I watch?"

"Yes, I'd like to, but I have no idea how."

"Well, Ken, maybe an atheist can help. Your right arm is a mess, and you probably can't even move it. But your left arm is just fine. Can you lift it for me? Good. Now make a fist. Good. Now open your hand. Wonderful. Now, tell me how you did it."

"What?"

"Just tell me how you closed and opened your left hand."

"Well, there are these muscles, see? They are here in my forearm. I learned all of their names, once upon a time, back in comparative anatomy ... though I'm guessing I wouldn't remember the names now even if I hadn't cracked my head. When those muscles pull, my fingers close up. When they relax and the other muscles on the back of my arm pull, my hand opens. There are nerves running from the muscles to my brain.

When my brain sends certain electrical and chemical signals to the muscles, they pull or relax. How's that?"

"You explained how your body did it. You didn't explain how *you* did it. You have explained some of the aspects of your body's doing what you tell it to. How much of that did you understand the first time you opened and closed that fist?"

"None. I was an infant."

"Exactly. You knew nothing of the physical mechanism. You didn't even know the names of the nerves and muscles. What does that tell you?"

"Moving my hand has nothing to do with knowing how?"

"Yes! That's it!" Dr. Teasdale beams so proudly that I feel as if I have really accomplished something. "You know something about nerves and muscles and bones. But nobody has the slightest idea how your mind heard me tell it to open your fist and then followed my direction. How your mind controls your body is still a great scientific mystery. The connection between you and all those electrical signals in the computer you call a brain is totally unknown. Even if we did know all the details of the operation, that knowledge is totally irrelevant to your ability to move. You expect your fist to open, and it does. Isn't that kind of an everyday miracle? Now, Ken, tell me how you improved your skills in opening and closing your hand, such as catching and throwing a ball. Did you study the anatomy involved? How did you develop those skills?"

"I just did it. I did it over and over, and somehow it got better and easier."

"Now do you see how inappropriate it was of you to ask how to do a spiritual healing?"

"You don't believe in any god, yet you do believe in spiritual healings, don't you?"

"Yes. And I think you are going to have one. Tell me again how you are going to do it."

"I guess I'm supposed to just do it—do it over and over as it gets better and easier."

"That's right, Ken. Don't worry about how. You chose to come back to life after a fatal fall. Now, you can do more. Do you want more coaching?"

"Are you a coach of miracle healings?" I can't keep a bemused tone out of my voice. Based on his enthusiasm and his lecturing abilities, I can suddenly imagine his tour bus going from hospital to hospital on his motivational speaking tour, aimed mainly at vegetables who are seemingly too far gone to listen.

"Actually, Ken, you are not my first. But your abilities seem very special, and I want to explore them. Maybe we can make a game of it. Maybe you don't yet realize what a great miracle of healing you are. Have you had any miraculous healings in your past?"

"Well, Doctor, when I was twelve I slipped on a mat and fell against a church door. Both my hands went through the glass windows, and my left wrist was badly slashed. The pain was unbearable. Somebody held my arm, and somebody else drove me to the hospital. I just screamed in pain. Then, the Mormon bishop and his counselors put their hands on my head and gave me a blessing. While they were blessing me, the pain suddenly stopped. It was a miracle."

"And, Ken, you didn't know how it worked. You just expected it."

"I guess so."

"Ken, this is great. You have had a miraculous healing, and you have convinced me that you are an amazing man just by being alive. Can we start with your right arm?"

"Sure. Do you think I can fix it? You might be a medical doctor, but you can't know how I feel. Your medicine is keeping me numb, but I can feel the cast on my right arm. I feel the straps around my head and the braces on my legs. I feel like a dead man kept alive by your silly machines. And you think I can fix it all? You've got more faith in nothing than most churchgoers have in God," I say emphatically.

"I think we both expect you to do something amazing," retorts Teasdale. "Remember, you thought of opening your left fist, and somehow your mind, nerves, muscles, and bones made it happen. Maybe you can think of more direct results. Think about the broken bones, the torn muscles, the cut skin and blood vessels in your right arm. You don't need to remember their names or anatomy. Just think about them. Now, you might not know exactly how they are supposed to look, but they know. Think about telling them to arrange themselves as they should be. Tell your bones to come together in the right way and form the necessary attachments. Tell all the damaged tissue to transform itself into healthy tissue. Tell the muscles to find their correct connections and attachments. Bring the nerves and blood vessels together. Tell the skin to mend itself and then evict the sutures. Are you following my directives?"

"Yes, Doctor," I reply, almost unconsciously.

"Good. Now, do it some more. Imagine all the parts of your arm, and tell them to be whole. Tell them to do three months of healing in three minutes. You are the king of the land. Your body is the land. All sixty trillion cells are your subjects. They have to obey your will. Will them to obey and heal." *Wow, this guy is good!* "Make it happen, Ken. Make it happen. Make it happen because you expect it to happen. Understand that you don't need to understand. It isn't how. It just is. Heal your arm. Heal your arm. Good. How do you feel?"

"Huh?" *I feel like I've been asleep.* "Oh, Dr. Teasdale, I'm beginning to think you might be the world's only atheistic faith healer."

"Please, Ken, call me Jim."

"Okay, Jim. I think I can feel my right arm. It hurts."

"That's expected. You can tell the pain to go away and fix all the problems on its way."

"You know, Jim, I think we have made progress. Look. I can lift my right arm. I can make a fist. Here, shake my hand."

"That's very good, Ken. Just a minute while I turn over the tape. You don't mind that I'm recording everything for science, do you?"

"Not as long as you remember to keep it a secret until I go to Israel."

"We'll see. Now, do you think you can transform that plaster cast into powder?"

"I never thought of that. Do you think I can?"

"Just a minute while I make sure the video camera is running. Okay. Yes, you can turn that cast into powder. Just imagine it is part of your body and therefore under your command. Why shouldn't the king of all of Canaan have royal powers over a lowly chunk of plaster? Just hold your arm out and tell the cast to fall to the floor as white powder and a little gauze. Okay, Ken—think, think. Tell all those plaster particles to let go of each other. Tell them to disband. Tell them the meeting is over and they can separate."

As Jim talks and I concentrate, the cast slowly softens and begins to fall like sand from my arm. The gauze slips away and a perfectly healthy right arm emerges. I am truly astonished. The spirit was right. It wasn't just a dream. I have one thought: *Wow!*

Jim gasps.

"Either these drugs are better than I thought," I croak, flexing my right hand painlessly and trying to decide whether I was hallucinating, "or I make one heck of a doctor."

With Jim's coaching, I repeat the healing process on my legs, feet, and back. Finally, we focus on my cranium and completely heal the bones and other injuries.

As the pain seeps away, I become more and more excited. I have never felt so alive, so vibrant. *I should have let some woman's crazy husband chase me off a roof years ago,* I think in wonder. I have gone from an invalid to a better version of my former self, complete with perfectly functional knees that haven't moved this smoothly since I played one too many games of tackle football.

"Ken, you have just made it virtually impossible for me to keep you a secret," Jim says as I touch my toes experimentally. "Why don't you give up the idea?"

"I think I know how to persuade you. How well do you see without those glasses?"

"Not very well."

"Do you mind closing your eyes?" I ask.

"No." Jim smiles faintly and obeys more readily than I expected. I guess no one argues with a miracle worker—or at least that's what I'm counting on.

"Okay, now take off your glasses and open your eyes."

"Oh, I can see perfectly!" exclaims Jim as he looks thoughtfully at his glasses. At first, he moves to tuck them into the pocket of his jacket. Then, he simply chucks them into the trash with a flourish. He looks at himself in the mirror and then smiles at me.

"Twenty-twenty vision, I believe. Now, here's the deal," I explain. "If you do everything you can to keep my secret, you keep your perfect eyesight. If you spill the beans, you wear the glasses again. How about it? Is it a deal?"

"I'll do my best," says Jim, "but I'm not sure your heart won't prevent you from harming my eyesight."

We survey one another and smile. Miracles can make friends out of a pair of strangers pretty quickly, I guess.

"Now comes the hard part," says Jim, getting serious. "We will need to document everything and keep it secret from the media. I don't know how I'm going to do that, since I refuse to lie outright. Let me see if I can move you to a more private room. I'll tell the staff we're doing experiments, and we need complete privacy. They don't have to know why. I think we can trust Dr. Jones. We certainly can't keep your healthy body from him. Maybe you could stay in bed with all those lines taped to your skin. I don't know, though. Keeping this private is going to be tough. You'll have to play dead for your visitors. If you pretend to be unconscious, you aren't lying. You won't be saying you can't talk. Of course it will give me time to prepare my reports without competition. On the other hand, a press conference tomorrow, New Year's Day, would sure be nice."

"I'll cooperate with you, Jim. But I'm not sick and shouldn't have to pay for any more tests or X-rays."

"Oh, don't worry. I've talked with my publisher, and he's taking care of your entire bill."

"That's good, since I opted for the cheapest insurance plan the hospital offers, ironically enough. I'd hate to have to give them all of my salary back!"

"If you can't afford decent health insurance, how do you expect to finance a trip to Israel?"

"I thought I would test my powers on the lottery."

"I'm not sure that wouldn't be unethical. Think about the consequences if the world discovered you used your powers that way. In the first place, it would destroy the lotto. In the second place, it might give your ego the upper hand. In the third place, people will be less willing to support your plans for peace. Oh, yes, they will think you somehow cheated for personal gain and are therefore unworthy to lead them. You better let me call my publisher about financing your trip. He trusts me, and I think I can convince him he's going to make millions for an investment of thousands. Oh, yes, Ken, I see a best-seller in the making, regardless of the outcome of your trip. I doubt it will cost as much as your medical bill. I think I'm beginning to see why so many of the world's great mystics were poor. We better keep you looking poor, like Gandhi."

"Thanks, Jim ... I think. You do believe we can make a difference for peace, don't you?"

"Sure, Ken, no problem," says Jim without conviction. "You helped me see better. Maybe you can help the Jews and Arabs see eye to eye." Jim rolls his eyes, clearly contemplating the enormity of the task. "It's a lot more than medical healing," he thinks aloud. "According to the story, Jesus's accomplishments were just as amazing as what you have done today, and Ken, they nailed the guy to a cross. I don't think political failure gets much more dramatic than that! How do you make peace without forcing people's minds?"

I don't respond, and Jim seems to figure out that he's arguing with a human wall of determination, so he just sighs and says, "Whatever you do, I expect to make a fortune being there and writing about it. Listen, in a few minutes it will be midnight. We will enter a new millennium. I just coached you through the fastest recovery of all time, and you just got the glasses restriction off my driver's license, so I'm thinking that makes us friends. At a time like this, it is traditional to drink a toast and kiss a friend. How about it if you change these two cups of water into cups of champagne for our toast?"

The water becomes champagne. We raise our cups and gently sip. It's surprisingly good. After kissing my cheek, European-style, Jim whispers in my ear, "I think you better forget about making wine from water in the future. This is the best champagne I have ever tasted, worth at least a hundred dollars a bottle. If this gets out, you will hurt a lot of innocent people in the wine industry. Won't that violate one of Santa's rules?"

Surprised, I jump back and demand, "How do you know about Santa's rules?"

"Remember Billy Mitchell, that boy who sat on your knee?"

"Yes, I remember him. How do you know his name?" I ask, feeling a bit like Billy must have felt. "I didn't tell you about him."

"Believe it or not, that little rascal was wired for sound. His friend a few yards away recorded your entire conversation. I guess Billy recorded a dozen or so other Santas before you. He intended it as a school project. When he recognized you in the news, Billy sold his tape to the *Deseret News* of Salt Lake City, and they published a transcript. Everyone in Utah knows how to break a candy cane and put a piece on Earth. That was very clever. I've never heard it before. Did you think it up?"

"Santa says some amazing things when I get out of his way. He's definitely much wiser than I am. I learn a lot every time I channel him."

"Perhaps you could explain to me what Santa meant when he said everything is imaginary."

"Maybe someday Santa can explain that to both of us, Jim."

"I see. So you aren't new to spiritual powers. You actually believe you channeled Santa?"

"Oh, I've channeled lots of people or been visited by them. I remember being visited by my grandmother's grandmother. She and her two young children were trapped by a blizzard in 1856 with some Mormon pioneers in a place called Martin Cove, Wyoming. She claimed I had been her guardian angel then, even if I couldn't remember it later, as a kindly spirit who helped her stay strong and keep her head for the sake of her children. Later, she repaid the favor, because once, on a SCUBA expedition, I was about ninety feet down when I heard my great-great-grandmother warning me to check my air. She saved me from a serious diving emergency. Yes, channeling is easy. But I'm certainly new to all this. I feel tired. Happy New Year, Jim."

"Happy new millennium, Ken."

Chapter VI

Convalescing

In THE DAYS THAT follow, I am transferred to a private room with new casts and phony connections. Family and friends still see me as a living corpse confined to my bed. Jim watches as a select few staff members perform multiple tests to fill "his" records.

I learn that part of the reason Jim is an atheist is the bitterness he felt when his Christian friends told him how much God hates homosexuality. In one interesting conversation, Jim tells me the similarity between homosexuality and hallucinogenic drugs:

"Homosexuality enables one to have the sexual experience without producing offspring. This is very offensive to the genetic code that wants so desperately to get itself into the next generation. So, we inherit taboos against homosexuality. Hallucinogenic drugs, on the other hand, enable a person to have the spiritual experience without religion. That lets the cat out of the bag. Religion is one way our genetic code ensures effective procreation. Without religion, we might not form useful communities. We might become promiscuous and make offspring before we are ready to raise them. Or, we might learn to enjoy our sexual urges in ways the code would not like. Thus, our genetic code gives us religion with a higher authority to keep us in line. So, homosexuality and hallucinogenic drugs are taboo for similar reasons—they provide the sexual or spiritual experience without producing the desired results."

Jim says he is sure homophobia and psychodelophobia are genetically inherited, and he doesn't blame those who can't overcome their natural urges to persecute gays and drug users. "I sure can't overcome my natural homosexual urges, and believe me, I've tried," he says with shrugged shoulders. Jim says he has tried LSD and "shrooms." "I think I found the same spiritual experience my religious friends find in church. I admit I can't be sure, since I haven't had any spiritual experiences in church or with God. I also decided that spiritual experience can include miraculous healings, hence my books."

I'm not sure about this guy—tolerant, yes; in need of tolerance, definitely. LDS (Mormon) and LSD (more fun) don't usually mix very well. I have never heard of a victim of intolerance who could be so understanding and tolerant.

Another time, Jim makes the political point that a group of friends could each bring their favorite dish to a party. One might sample every dish and find some good, some indifferent, and some downright offensive. Then he asks why the government shouldn't vote on which dishes may or may not be eaten. President Bush certainly would have vetoed any law allowing broccoli. I agree with Jim that laws against victimless personal practices, such as homosexuality and drugs, are just as inappropriate as laws against unappetizing foods.

"I hope the world tolerates your powers more than it tolerates gays and drugs," he summarizes. "I fear they won't. Either way, I'm looking at a best-seller, and the world can go to hell. They don't deserve either of us."

Jim surprises me with his influence and ability to convince the hospital authorities to release me under his supervision. Although I'm in great shape, the hospital agrees to pretend I'm comatose and useless for anything but Jim's scientific research. I suspect it has something to do with the million dollars his publishers donated to the hospital.

Jim takes me to his research facility in Chicago. Actually, the special facility is a suite on the second floor of his apartment building. It's very nice, and I get my own room. Jim provides me with everything I ask, including spending money. I'm free to come and go as I please. I learn a lot about the various forms of entertainment in Chicago. My younger brother has contacted and agrees to keep my secret. I spend a lot of time with him and his family in his luxury Chicago mansion.

Being in Chicago allows us to continue keeping me a secret and will enable me to leave the country without raising questions in Utah. Nearly everyone in Utah still thinks I am in an endless coma. My children gave up on me when they allowed my body to be shipped out of state. They admitted that I, being a medical researcher, would have wanted my body to serve science, even after my mind was gone.

I'm sorry they don't know I'm awake, but I can't risk my mission to Israel. I realize this temporary deception, even of family and friends, is worth the hope of achieving my mission, but it isn't easy to think about. The children I raised, whom I love more than anything, are convinced I'll never speak to them again; they think they've said one of the hardest good-byes they could say. I tell myself that their grief is all the more reason to get the job done quickly and decisively.

Having to choose between one's children and the fate of the world is harder than it looks, though. Despite myself, I think of the days when I would tuck my oldest daughter in at night.

"Stay, Daddy," she would always insist, unable to fall asleep unless I promised not to walk away from her and leave her in the dark. I never had to sit there long, though; she would fall asleep before I could finish a book, once she knew I wasn't going anywhere.

A lump rises in my throat. When all of this is over, I only hope my kids will understand how my love and hope for the world justifies the deception. I miss the rest of my siblings, my children and grandchildren, and my many friends back home.

Chapter VII

TV

Jim AGREES THAT WE should have our own news coverage of our trip to Israel. He has a friend who would be perfect. Her name is Marsha Clark. She is a TV anchorwoman in Chicago. She has done other stories on amazing healings with Jim, and he trusts that she will keep our secret. Israel is ready to explode any day. Our only chance of getting to Israel now is to go as part of Marsha Clark's news staff. This is going to take some convincing. Jim takes me to the TV studio.

From the looks of her private office, Marsha must be very important. She has a glass-topped desk in front of a bay window, flanked by shelves full of Marsha's broadcasting awards. Several overstuffed chairs and an antique coffee table fill the space before her desk. Marsha herself is even more formally attired than her office. She is obviously Scandinavian, with trimmed blonde hair and high cheekbones. Her body is as carefully sculptured as her face, suggesting some kind of regular athletic activity. She fills her suit very well. She appears glad to see Jim again and offers us a drink as we sit together.

"Marsha, this is Ken," Jim says, "the man I told you about."

"Hello, Marsha. I'm pleased to meet you." I shake her hand.

"Hi, Ken. And Jim, you say this man should be dead?" Marsha wears a skeptical grin as she sips her coffee.

"Before going any further," says Jim, "I must have your strict agreement to confidentiality."

Mockingly, Marsha raises her right hand. "I so swear. Now, what have you got that requires an oath? You have never requested that of me before."

"Just let me put this video into your VCR, and I think you will be very impressed."

Marsha watches the video and sees the cast fall from my arm. She clearly struggles to maintain the neutral expression of a disinterested journalist before giving in to her surprise. "Wow!" she finally says. "That's really impressive. Either you have some great technology or this guy is real."

"Listen, Marsha, Ken thinks he can go to Israel and make peace. I know it sounds impossible, but this guy does the impossible. I believe him, and I think he can make you believe as well. Before we show you any more, we needed you to promise that nothing will leak out before we all arrive in Israel."

"We *all*?" asks Marsha, rather surprised. "I thought you would want to do a story here."

"Yes, Marsha, we are going to Israel," says Jim. "I couldn't tell you about that before gaining your confidentiality. We've got all the financial support necessary, but we need you."

"Well," says Marsha, "I'm willing to play along if you really think there's a story."

"Marsha," says Jim, "this has the potential of being the story of your life. Trust me."

Marsha nods, but she seems skeptical.

Jim continues. "Do you have an executive officer who will authorize our trip off the record? My publisher will pay everything, including salaries, but we will fail if our purpose is exposed. We must go as a news team."

"That would be Mr. Sands," replies Marsha.

"If you invite him into your office, I think Ken can convince him to cooperate. Do we have a deal?"

"Why not? It sounds exciting," says Marsha as she crosses her arms and raises her eyebrows, indicating a strange mixture of trust and disbelief. "Even if this man is a fraud, it might make a newsworthy story."

Marsha and Jim step out of her office and into Mr. Sands's next door. I can hear their hushed conversation. Marsha vouches for Jim's trustworthiness without being sure about me. Jim vouches for my powers. Soon, Mr. Sands has heard enough to pique his curiosity and get his promise of silence. They bring him to Marsha's room. He is over six feet tall and slightly balding. His moustache is perfectly trimmed and complements his bold chin. He speaks with authority, and firmly shakes our hands. He understands that we want to accompany Miss Clark and her camera crew to Israel on our own secret mission. His agreement to secrecy is based on one condition: that we can convince him we have something real, something more than sleight of hand. Marsha rolls her eyes to indicate to Mr. Sands that I am on my own. Jim handles the entire negotiation.

"Mr. Sands, I appreciate that you are a busy man. You don't have time to waste, and neither do we. We are very serious about our proposal. This is not a joke. I am so confident in this man's powers that I want you to ask him to perform a miracle—something that will convince you to cooperate. Pick anything. Just don't ask him to cause harm, to control the behavior of another human, or to create wealth. A simple parlor trick should suffice."

Mr. Sands ponders the request for a minute. He sets a standard to test our claim. "I want a cameraman who can go with you to come in now and video the entire event. Marsha, how about Gary Clayton?" In a few minutes a little fat man enters and sets up his camera. Once the camera is rolling, Mr. Sands makes his request. "Ken, I want you to float up to that light fixture and break it with your bare hands. Then I want you to return to the floor and stand here next to me while the pieces of broken glass float back up to the ceiling, reform, and make light again."

Jim nods reassuringly, and I think about floating. As I slowly rise in the air, Mr. Sands runs around me to check for wires. The camera records everything as I approach the light fixture. I grasp it in my hands and squeeze gently. It explodes and falls to the floor in a thousand sharp pieces. I return to the floor and step next to Mr. Sands. I notice a small cut on my left palm and think it better. From the way his mouth drops open, I know that Mr. Sands has seen my palm heal itself. I talk to the broken glass, and it hears me. It returns to the ceiling, assumes its former shape, and illuminates the room again. Clayton, the cameraman, is too stunned to turn off the camera. Everyone stands quietly for a few moments until Jim nudges Clayton to stop recording.

We all look at Mr. Sands. His mouth is agape, and his

arms are hanging limply at his sides. After recovering from his shock, Mr. Sands asks Marsha to invite David Brown, her best producer, into the room to observe the videotape and verify his observations. David describes the same scene on tape that the others saw minutes before. Mr. Sands tells him that he is going to Israel with us. We have our television crew. Everyone agrees to secrecy. Jim and I are supplied with press passes, and we are now part of a news team on its way to Israel to cover a war.

I pat my pockets and realize that my passport and visa forms have appeared there. Ah, well, just another miracle on today's agenda, apparently. I have a feeling this new knack of mine is going to come in pretty handy.

Chapter VIII

If Frogs Could Fly

OUR FIRST FLIGHT IS to New York, where we catch a trans-Atlantic flight on Air France to Paris. As we sit down, I notice the seats are smaller and less comfortable than our previous flight on United. Those of us with a few extra pounds notice such things. I see familiar name tags on the shirts of the two young men seated next to me: Elder Smith and Elder Young. Below each name is written *L'Eglise de Jesus Christ des Saints des Dernier Jours*. They are Mormons.

"Bonjour," I say. "Il-y-a presque quarante ans depuis mon départ pour ma mission en France."

"Vraiment?" says Elder Smith, rolling his "r" astonishingly well as he expresses his surprise.

I continue in my best French. "Oui, J'ai servi dans les missions Francais de l'Est et Franco-Belge."

"Nous allons a la mission Paris Sud," says Elder Young in broken French.

"Merveilliex!" I exclaim. "J'ai tellmont de bon memoirs de ma mission. Je vous envie."

Jim interrupts to introduce himself and move the conversation into English. "So tell me, are you guys related to your famous namesakes?"

"Are you referring to Joseph Smith and Brigham Young, the first two Mormon prophets?" I ask. "You certainly know your Mormon history, don't you?"

"Well," says Jim, "we atheists probably know more about religious history than most believers."

"Actually," says Elder Young, "we are both direct descendants of our namesake prophets."

"You must carry a terrific burden," says Jim. "I guess everyone will expect your ancestries to enable both of you to find more Mormon converts than usual."

"Yes," responds Elder Smith, "it is a heavy burden to bear." His smooth forehead creases with responsibility beyond his years, but his pleasant smile doesn't disappear.

"Don't worry," I add, "whatever anyone else expects, God only expects you to be yourselves and do your personal best. He will not hold you to any higher standard than he held me, an unknown."

"You know, you are the first person to put it that way. Thank you," says Elder Smith.

"You give them comfort talking about a God who has no more evidence than the Tooth Fairy," says Jim.

"Don't worry about my friend here," I say to the young men. "I think he's as much against religion as he is for atheism. I think he puts God on a par with the Tooth Fairy, Santa Claus, and the Easter Bunny."

"I'm not sure Ken here is still a Mormon," says Jim to the men. "And why shouldn't we compare God with Santa?"

"Listen, Jim," I say, "when these young men go to France they will speak to the people in French. When I want to speak to them about spiritual matters, I speak Mormon because that's their spiritual language. Never mind that these days, I believe that there is validity in all faiths, including your atheism."

"Wait a minute," says Elder Young. "Are you two making fun of us?" I suspect he wouldn't be surprised if we were.

"Would you be making fun of a French person by speaking French to them?" I ask.

"No, but that's different," says Smith.

"How is it different?" I respond.

"How is it the same?" challenges Smith.

"Let me show with an example. When I hear the word *grenouille*—Jim, that's French for 'frog'—I see a green amphibian with long legs that catches flies with its tongue. I don't see the English word 'frog.' It won't be long before you have that kind of familiarity with French. Now, tell me. Which is more correct, the French word grenouille or the English word frog?"

"It depends on whether you are in France or America," Elder Smith says after a thoughtful pause.

"Yes," I continue, "and when a frog is looking for a mate, does he think about a grenouille or a frog?"

"Frogs don't use either word," says Elder Young. "They don't have language."

"Obviously, Elder Young, you have never been near a swamp at night," I say, asserting my authority as an avid herpetologist. "They use a very sophisticated language to find the right mate. Every species has a specific croak that appeals to females of their own kind. Animals have language and mating rituals to keep them within their own species. Likewise, humans have specific language, customs, and religious beliefs and rituals to keep them within their own groups. You will speak French to the French and English to the English. And if you want to speak to a Russian, you will learn Russian or find someone who can translate for you. So why shouldn't I speak Mormon to a Mormon and Catholic to a Catholic? We have a word for 'frog' in every language. They are all different, and they are all useful for human communication, while none of them is recognizable to the frogs. And just as the frogs use their own language, I suspect God's celestial friends never use any of our human terms for Him. Yet He answers our prayers no matter which word we use to address Him."

"Careful, Ken, you're beginning to sound like me," laughs Jim with a grin and the best bow he can manage in an airplane seat.

"I see your point about language," says Elder Smith. "Everyone knows words are just symbols. But God is real. He is not just a symbol or some abstract idea. The truth about God is something we discover and learn, not something we invent."

As he listens to his friend speak, Elder Young radiates spiritual conviction and appears to be moving into a spiritual trance.

I ignore Smith's testimony. "Do you expect to teach English while you are in France?" I ask candidly.

"I suppose we will," says Elder Smith. Then he reaches over and tugs gently on Elder Young's sleeve to bring him down from his celestial meditations. Elder Young nods and smiles.

"I taught both Mormonism and English when I was a Mormon missionary," I say. "We taught English in hopes of finding friends to whom we could preach our beliefs. Some of the French were grateful for the help in English, and some were grateful for the help in Mormonism. In both cases, they learned useful tools for their lives."

"If you see Mormonism as just another tool for spirituality, why bother teaching it?" asks Elder Young with his palms up.

"Do you see the advantage of going out in pairs?" I say to Jim. "One is thinking while the other is speaking. It gives them a great advantage over most of us who cannot think while talking. I think we're sitting next to a couple of great missionaries. The church is in good hands with them."

"Do you think we might be a pair of missionaries for peace?" suggests Jim. Everyone chuckles at Jim's clever question. I nod in agreement. The missionaries are a bit confused at such a claim.

"I will explain our mission for peace in a minute," I say, "but first I want to explore Elder Young's question. Many of the people in the world, including France, have not had a satisfactory spiritual experience in their own culture and religion. You talk to them about Mormonism and raise some questions. They are motivated to get their own spiritual experience. They have their experience while seeking the truth about Mormonism. That experience is very valuable, and you helped them achieve it. They join the Mormon Church and continue to have pleasant spiritual experiences that they did not have before. They are happy. Their spiritual powers are enhanced. You have helped them find a priceless inner source. They are grateful for the rest of their lives. You, too, will have wonderful and powerful spiritual experiences with these French converts as they share their stories with you. You have a wonderful mission to accomplish. I'm just saying that you could preach Buddha with the same power and get the same wonderful results."

"Bravo!" Jim applauds. "I have a convert."

"Not so fast," I contend. "You aren't willing to believe in any God, and I'm willing to believe in them all. That's how we are different."

"No, Ken," says Jim with an air of superiority, "that's how we are the same."

"I'm confused," says Elder Smith.

Elder Young fidgets with an empty bag of peanuts. I can't tell whether he's becoming bored with the conversation or becoming concerned that a new holy war is going to break out in our aisle.

"That's wonderful," I respond, "now you have a question for the Spirit. You will take your question to the Lord, and you will have a spiritual experience. You will have more spiritual power the next time you bear your personal witness that the Mormon Church is true. People will feel your power and seek their own spirituality because of you. Stay confused. Stay in the question. Keep asking. The answers don't matter. What matters is the power and experience you receive as you get your answers. If you can convince anyone to get into their spirit, you will have your victory. What they get from the Spirit and what they do with it will be their victory or failure, not yours. Mormonism has a wonderful concept in the idea that you can't get to heaven on a borrowed testimony. You have to get your own spiritual confirmation. I really like that belief. I think they lose it when they suggest that the only valid testimony is one that supports your belief in the borrowed beliefs of others. The Ninth Article of Faith says Mormons believe additional doctrines are yet to be revealed. Why can't you get them on your own, without waiting for the rest of the church?"

"I think I'm even more confused," confesses Elder Smith.

"Wonderful," I applaud. "Tell me, Elder Smith, how long did it take you to learn French?"

"Six weeks in the Missionary Training Center."

"Did you hear that, Jim? This young man just spent six weeks learning to speak conversational French and memorizing his religious lessons in that French. Wouldn't you call that a miracle? Jim, here, is an expert on spiritual miracles, and maybe he understands something about linguistic miracles."

"Well, Ken," responds Jim, "I'm no expert on linguistics, but I can't imagine anyone making himself understood very well in a foreign language after only six weeks. Yes, maybe I need to do some research with Mormon missionary language training. Maybe we're looking at a chapter in a future book."

"Good idea," I say. "Personally, I'm convinced that my French came to me with the aid of the Spirit. I went on my mission before they had the missionary training center. I had a year of high school French and a year of college French. I didn't know much at all, but within six weeks of arriving in France I was talking about religion in French. By the end of my mission, people believed I was from France because I had lost my American accent. I give the Spirit, whatever it is, credit."

"We talk a lot about the gift of languages," says Elder Young. "One of our Articles of Faith says we believe in the gift of tongues. I would say that gift is a common occurrence at the Missionary Training Center."

"You get it because you expect it," says Jim.

"We get it because we believe the story in the Bible that says when Peter spoke on the day of Pentecost, everyone heard him in their own language," insists Smith with youthful stubbornness. "Why shouldn't God be willing to do that miracle today for all the Mormon missionaries who believe?"

"I believe you can learn languages miraculously," says Jim. "You are proof of that. I've seen greater miracles." He turns and winks at me. "I just don't see any evidence that some external God did it for you."

"Jim believes he is an atheist, like I said," I add. I try my own logic. "Let me put it this way: you are climbing a mountain. At the base, you see dozens of trailheads. You wonder which is best. Some of the trails are long and boring; some are exciting and adventurous. One goes straight up a vertical cliff. You pick a trail and hike to the top. As you reach the top, you suddenly see the other side of the mountain. You see both sides—yin and yang, good and evil, Christ and Satan, all at the same time. Suddenly, you see the oneness of it all. With all your awareness, however, you still can't tell another climber which trail will be best for him. That's for him to decide. We each pick our own trail, based on our skills and preferences. Yet we all strive for the same peak. So many different trails, yet the last step of each is the same."

"Isn't it possible," says Elder Smith slowly, "that some trails don't go to the top? Isn't it possible that you can be deceived into dead-end trails? Isn't it best to find a trail you know will take you to the right peak? We believe we can point people to that trail."

"Yes," I respond, "I'm sure there are plenty of trails that don't make it. Even Mormonism won't take you to the top if you don't keep on keeping on."

"We call it enduring to the end," adds Elder Young.

"You do believe Moses and his people were led by God, don't you?" I ask.

"Of course," says Smith. "Moses was a true prophet."

"But wouldn't you agree that the theocracy under Moses was very different from Mormonism today?" I ask. "You don't burn witches or stone adulteresses. You don't kill a chicken for God or circumcise your boys. Didn't they walk a different path from you, and couldn't they get to the same destination? My point is that not that all trails are true, only that there might be more than one true trail."

"Maybe so," responds Smith, "but God would never confuse people with two different true churches at the same time."

"I'm reminded of a SCUBA vacation I took to Cancun, Mexico," I say. "We visited the ruins at Chichen Itza. A member of our group and I climbed what appeared to be the front slope of the highest pyramid. At the top, we explored the temple and saw that all four sides came to the same top. Each side had its own top, yet there was only one top. We saw our friends climbing the back side. I didn't tell them they were on the wrong staircase, even though they were on a different side from the one I had ascended. I stood at the top of their side and shouted mock encouragement, things like, 'If you slip, you will die.'"

"Great encouragement," Jim interrupts with a chuckle.

I continue. "Once on top of the pyramid, you realize that the four different sides are part of a single whole, and you can shout down any side to those climbing it. No matter what spiritual trail you take, when you reach the top you will be at the top of all other spiritual trails. You will be fluent in all spiritual languages. That awareness is like opening your eyes. Did you ever notice the Great Seal of the United States? It's printed on the back of a one-dollar bill." As I speak, the missionaries reach for dollar bills from their wallets. "Our slogan is *E Pluribus Unum*—out of many, one. It is symbolized by a pyramid, a structure with four sides, all leading to a single top. When you reach the top, you become aware. That awareness is symbolized by the all-seeing eye above the pyramid. Besides seeing the land all around, you see some ideas you hadn't supposed. If you pay attention, you can find God's clues in practically everything, even Jim's atheism."

Silently, the missionaries stuff their dollars back in their wallets.

"Let me take this conversation to a new level," says Jim. "Ken told me he had his first kiss after his mission. Is that going to be the case with either of you?"

Somewhat embarrassed by the question, the two young men exchange sheepish glances and decide to admit that they both already have had a first kiss.

"I didn't mean to probe into your personal lives," says Jim. "I just want to compare religion with sex. Most people, when having sex, fantasize. They enhance their partner's sexuality. A man imagines his partner has bigger bosoms. A woman imagines her partner is better endowed, or he actually loves her. Fantasy is an important part of sex. During sex, humans use their brains to enhance the experience. They know the fantasy is not real; they don't care. They also know that some fantasies work better than others. Whichever fantasy turns you on is right for you. You don't deny yourself the pleasures of a good sexual fantasy just because it isn't real. You might share your sexual fantasies with another. If you write about it or produce it in a movie, it's called pornography. You might learn new and better fantasies from pornography, but you would never think of telling someone that your favorite fantasy is the only true fantasy or that he must imagine it when having sex or he will be wrong."

The missionaries squirm and roll their eyes at each other. I begin to feel uncomfortable for them.

Jim goes on, "Likewise, theology is useful for enhancing the spiritual experience. Different theologies work better for different people. Maybe it's all cultural. Maybe some of it is genetic, like the mating rituals of Ken's frogs. You go to France and teach people the Mormon theology. If it works for them to enhance their spirituality, they adopt it. You have done them a great service, just as the pornographer serves those whose sexuality is enhanced. Your sexual fantasies are not real, yet they serve you. Why do you need to believe your theology is real? In science, we have no truths. May I suggest a new definition for the word 'truth'? Why not say something is true if it works. If Mormonism enhances your spiritual powers, then it is true. If you go to God in prayer about your church, and you have a wonderful spiritual experience, then your church is true. It is true because it works. And later, after your mission, when you get married, you will learn which sexual fantasies are true for you. I would not tell you that your imaginary God is the wrong God for you any more than I would tell you that your imaginary sex partner is the wrong fantasy for you."

Judging from the red tinge creeping up from their collars, I wonder if sex is a good subject for two young missionaries. Jim pushes even harder.

"On the other hand," says Jim, "even the best fantasies should never substitute for action, whether spiritual or sexual. Far too many people watch porn when they should be developing their sexual powers. And too many people read holy books when they should be enhancing their spiritual powers. Pornography is most useful for people who are unable to enjoy their own sexual powers or relate to a partner, and religion is most useful for people who are unable to enjoy their own spiritual powers. If your sex is unsatisfactory, maybe it's your partner. Likewise, if your spirituality needs help, maybe—"

"Right now," I interrupt hastily, eager to take control of the discussion before it gets even more awkward, "you will be very successful if you can learn the simple lesson that spiritual experiences can be a substitute for sexual experiences. Every time you feel tempted to enjoy a sexual fantasy, switch gears and learn that you can have pleasure with a spiritual experience. I guarantee to you that the Holy Ghost can give you enough spiritual pleasure to keep you in a state of spiritual euphoria sufficient to help you resist anything you might enjoy sexually. Leave the girls alone. Leave yourself alone. Turn your mind to the Spirit, but not because it is a duty or a commandment, or because you fear condemnation from God or men. Rather, do it because a good spiritual experience can be better than sex."

"Now, I'm really confused," says Elder Smith.

"Your mind is confused," I answer. "Your spirit understands perfectly. Get out of your mind and spend the next two years in your spirit. You will be wonderful missionaries. Both of you will. I predict you will find your spiritual assurance and exceed the expectations of your namesakes, both of you."

Everyone is silent as we finish our meals and ponder our conversations.

Suddenly, we are interrupted by the airplane speaker. "Ladies and gentlemen, we are beginning our descent to Charles de Gaulle International Airport in Paris. Please return to your seats and give your trays to the attendants as they come down the aisle."

"My, how time flies when you're confused," concludes Jim, very pleased by the conversation.

"So," asks Young, "what are you going to do in France? How do you intend to be missionaries for peace?"

"You remembered!" I exclaim. "We're going on to Israel."

Jim pipes up, "That's all we can say. Please don't mention this before Easter. That might put us at risk."

"Your secret is safe with us," says Smith. "Good luck kicking Palestinian butt. You don't happen to have a few nuclear missiles up your sleeve, do you?"

"Oh," I reply sincerely, "we are going to make peace, not war."

"So what are you going to do?" asks Young. "Tell them they should just be friends? Maybe you should practice by getting my dog and cat to live peacefully." He winks at Smith.

"Yeah, something like that," I say, unperturbed. "If we are successful, you will hear about it."

"God be with you," says Smith, rolling his eyes at Young. Both missionaries appear relieved that Jim and I are not to be taken seriously.

"You too," I respond.

Chapter IX

The French Connection

We are part of the madness at Charles de Gaulle International Airport. Approaching El Al, the Israeli airline, in the concourse, we see a lot of commotion. We learn that the entire Palestinian diplomatic corps is leaving Paris because of the military tensions in Israel. About two dozen Muslim Arabs will fly with us. I suddenly feel inspired to look like a Muslim. I step up to one of the Muslims and tell him, in my best French, that I want to look just like him. We strike a deal—I offer him five hundred dollars, which I get from Jim—and the Muslim and I go to the restroom and exchange clothes. Jim is astonished and amused. I assure him that his five hundred was well spent. The Muslim is roundly teased by his comrades when he joins them again, wearing my clothes. Marsha decides to interview me on camera, although she has agreed not to release the interview just yet. The Muslims watch with interest as they see a strange American in Muslim attire being interviewed by an American TV reporter.

We are on El Al, Israeli Airlines Flight 666. I ask the

attendant about the flight number, and she laughingly explains that this flight is preferred by Jewish businessmen. "Somehow, the Christian tourists always schedule a different flight," she says wryly, winking at me. The seats are even less comfortable than they were on Air France. The flight attendants are polite but cautious with their Muslim passengers. There is an obvious air of tension between the Israelis and Palestinians. Nobody is certain of when or if open warfare might break out. Conversations are subdued.

I find myself seated next to a white-bearded, energetic gentleman, probably in his sixties. His turban is lavish, with a ruby attached on the front. He introduces himself as the Palestinian ambassador to France. I suspect my powers are making seating arrangements. Ambassador Haddam turns to me and asks why I am dressed as a Muslim. He speaks politely but with authority. Although my French is pretty good, his English is much better.

"I am going to Israel as a Palestinian," I answer.

"Why?" Haddam asks.

"Because I believe I can help."

"How?"

"I have some important things to say," I respond with confidence.

"How will you say them?" asks Haddam. "Most Palestinians speak Arabic. Do you have a good translator?"

"No. If Allah wants me to help, he will provide."

"What do you know about Allah?" the ambassador challenges, shifting toward me in his seat.

Silently, I remember hugging Allah after my accident. In my mind, I see him winking. I acknowledge his wink and step aside. "I have read the Koran, and the Spirit has touched me. Perhaps you are familiar with this passage from the 'Table': 'And when they hear that which hath been sent down to the apostle read unto them, thou shalt see their eyes overflow with tears, because of the truth which they perceive therein, saying, O Lord, we believe; write us down therefore with those who bear witness to the truth: and what should hinder us from believing in God, and the truth which hath come unto us, and from earnestly desiring that our Lord would introduce us into paradise with the righteous people?'" I pause. "I have received the truths in the Koran. I have had the tears flow from my eyes. What should hinder me from believing?"

I look up into the silence. Ambassador Haddam and several Muslims within earshot are silently sobbing. Jim has a look of astonishment. Marsha is signaling to Gary, her cameraman.

"*Al-hamdulillah!*" cries Ambassador Haddam, which means "Praise the Lord!"

"Al-hamdulillah!" echo several others.

"Never," sobs Haddam, "never in my life have I heard the Koran quoted so eloquently. I thought I heard the Prophet himself, peace be upon him. Where did you learn to speak Arabic so perfectly? I wish I could read the Koran as well."

"Al-hamdulillah," I repeat softly. "Al-hamdulillah."

Ambassador Haddam raises his voice and faces the camera. "Ladies and gentlemen, we have received a witness from Allah. Allah has sent this man to rescue our people from oppression. I will be honored to be his humble servant. My entire staff and I shall devote ourselves to him. Al-hamdulillah!"

"Al-hamdulillah!" echoes throughout the plane.

"How can I serve you?" asks Haddam.

"I want to address the Palestinian leadership. Can you arrange it?"

After a gesture from Haddam, a secretary rushes to the cockpit to send an urgent message. "We will be met at the airport and taken to Palestinian headquarters. There is a war conference tomorrow. We are planning our strategy for victory. You will be the first to address the meeting. I will personally introduce you to President Arafat. You and your staff will be lodged as well as we can provide. I see you have reporters with you. They will be welcome until we begin our strategic plans. If there is anything else I can do for you, please don't hesitate to ask. Now, do you think you could cite a few more words from the Holy Book?"

"If Allah is willing. This is from the 'Bee':

"Unto God alone is the secret of heaven and earth known. And the business of the last hour shall be only as the twinkling of an eye, or even more quick: for God is almighty ... And God hath provided for you, of that which he hath created, conveniences to shade you from the sun, and he hath also provided you places of retreat in the mountains, and he hath given you garments to defend you from the heat, and coats of mail to defend you in your wars. Thus doth he accomplish his favor towards you, that ye may resign yourselves unto him. But if they turn back; verily thy duty is public preaching only. They acknowledge the goodness of God, and afterwards they deny the same; but the greater part of them are unbelievers. On a certain day we will raise a witness out of every nation: then they who shall have been unbelievers shall not be suffered to excuse themselves, neither shall they be received unto favor ... On a certain day we will raise up in every nation a witness against them, from among themselves; and we will bring thee, O Mohammed, as a witness against these Arabians. We have set down unto thee the book of the Koran, for an explication of everything necessary both as to faith and practice, and a direction, and mercy, and good tidings unto the Muslims. Verily God commandeth justice, and the doing of good, and the giving unto kindred what shall be necessary; and he forbiddeth wickedness, and iniquity, and oppression: he admonisheth you that ye may remember. Perform your covenant with God, when ye enter into covenant with him and violate not your oaths, after the ratification thereof; since ye have made God a witness over you. Verily, God knoweth that which ye do. And be not like unto her who undoeth that which she hath spun, untwisting it after she hath twisted it strongly; taking your oaths between you deceitfully because one party is more numerous than another party.'

"Have I not recited the secret to peace?" I ask.

One of the Israelis whispers to another, "I had no idea the Koran was in Hebrew."

"Neither did I." says the other.

I imagine I see Jehovah and Allah slapping hands and winking at me. Somehow, the tension on the plane is gone and hope begins to grow.

Chapter X

In the Belly of the Beast

THE ISRAELI AIRPORT IS like a military camp. Armed guards stand within a yard of each other. Every passenger is searched. Papers are examined thoroughly. Several Jewish passengers smile conspiratorially at us. We are loaded into vans and headed for Palestinian headquarters.

I had no idea the Palestinians could afford such a headquarters. It resembles a plain white building on the outside. It is deceptive. The inside resembles a lavish hotel with a grand hall. Ambassador Haddam is true to his word. We are graciously received at the Palestinian seat of government. We meet most of the leadership. President Arafat will arrive tomorrow. We retire to our upper-level rooms early, and I begin to focus on healing our jet lag. Jim and I share a suite, while our staff shares another.

We have barely unpacked when we hear a knock at our door. I open the door and see two beautiful women—one as white as snow, the other as black as coal. The beauty in their faces shows through their sheer veils. Their snug robes plainly reveal their curvaceous bodies. They ask if there is anything they can do to add to our comfort.

"Ha-ha," Jim laughs. "You don't want to give me any pleasure. If you do manage to turn me on, I'll be fantasizing about another man."

"Please, sir, forgive us. We mean nothing. And we will keep your secret from the authorities."

"Why?"

"Oh, excuse us, sir. If your preference is discovered, you will be banned."

"Why?"

"Allah has forbidden a man to be with a man."

"Why?"

The women exchange pained looks. "Oh, this is terrible! We didn't realize you didn't know. We don't know why. It is just very evil, and we must not talk of it anymore."

"Well, Ken, there you are," says Jim triumphantly. "You expect to help these people learn tolerance with the Jews and yet even their prostitutes can't tolerate a lifestyle like mine. Heh-heh. Listen, I'm going into the other room. You people do whatever you like. At least I'm tolerant. In fact, ladies, I'm even tolerant of intolerance. Heh-heh." Jim turns to me. "Here's another one for you, Ken. A lot of American women would complain about Muslim laws that make the women veil their faces in public—they say it is the establishment of religion. Then, those same American women expect their own government to force women to cover their nipples when dancing at a bar. Isn't it just as much the establishment of majority religious values when American communities force women to cover certain parts of their bodies in public as it is when Islamic governments force women to cover their faces? I'm just pointing out how hypocritical Americans are when they complain of religious laws in other countries. I hope you've got some real miracles up your sleeve. We've got four thousand years of intolerant traditions to overturn. And it appears that the disease of intolerance is pretty well universal. If I believed in God, I'd be praying for you tonight. Good night."

Jim closes the door behind him, and the black woman addresses me.

"Oh, sir. Please excuse us. We meant no offense. We are only here to offer ourselves for pleasure."

I stand before two very beautiful, smiling women. I think of Sandy and how lonely I have been. I wonder if the Spirit will mind if I enjoy the hospitality of my host. I wonder what these two women have in mind. I wonder if my family and friends will judge me. I wonder how I'm going to teach tolerance if I'm afraid of a little intolerance. I ask the women their names.

"I'm Yin, and this is Yang," says the black woman.

"Please do not worry about causing offense," says Yang. "You can choose either of us."

"When faced with an alternative," I respond, "a good friend of mine always says yes to both."

"I like your friend," says Yin.

I believe some mystic once said there is great joy in knowing yin and yang simultaneously. He was right.

Chapter XI

You Only Die Twice

A GENTLE SPRING RAIN greets us in the morning as we stroll from our barracks to the mess hall. The streets are empty, except for military guards who eye us with suspicion. Like any military mess hall, it is efficient but austere; crowded with guards but full of smiling cooks and friendly men from the plane. We eat together before the meeting. Jim turns to me while sipping his morning coffee.

"Ah, Ken," he says, smacking his lips over his coffee, "how did you like your Doublemint twins?"

"Actually, Jim, I learned quite a bit."

"Please ..." Jim holds up his hand. "Spare me the details."

"Okay, Jim, no details. But I had no idea there were so many ways to enjoy the pleasures of the flesh."

"You know, Ken," says Jim, "you and I treat women the same way we treat gods."

"*What?*" I exclaim. "I can't wait to hear your explanation."

"It's really quite simple, Ken. With regard to women and gods, you choose all, and I choose none."

From the smile curling around the lip of his coffee cup, I can tell he couldn't wait to deliver that particular line, but I have to laugh. Jim's arguments can be annoying at times, but they were also somewhat endearing, now that I'd met some new lady friends and gotten some sleep. "I guess that makes us opposites."

"Yes, Ken, opposite and the same. You see, we both have the method for peace. We both refuse to choose among alternatives. For example, when the atheistic Communists ruled Yugoslavia, they rejected all religions. So the Serbs, Croats, and Muslims lived side by side as peaceful victims. Now, they are killing each other to decide which culture will control the others. In America, the government is forbidden from taking sides. All cultures are accepted. Serbs, Croats, and Muslims can live in New York City and enjoy the same peace they had under Communism. When there is an alternative, you have four choices. You can pick choice A, choice B, both, or neither. It appears to me that Yin and Yang are at peace concerning you and me. They agree to dislike me, and they agree to like you. In both cases, they are at peace. Peace has many faces."

"That's very interesting," I say. "I think when it comes to women and gods, I prefer my approach."

"Of course you do," says Jim. "I'm just pointing out that we are the flip sides of the same coin of peace." Jim sets his coffee cup on a table by the door. "You don't seem pleased with my observation that we are so similar in our oppositeness."

"I'm not displeased. I'm just contemplating the thought," I say as we leave the mess hall for the meeting hall.

Again, we are searched and our papers examined. The meeting hall is considerably grander than the cafeteria-type room where we had eaten that morning. It looks like about a hundred Palestinian officers and soldiers are seated on rows of chairs. As we enter the hall, a hush of respectful nods greets us. We sense an air of tension and anticipation. Up front is a table surrounded by flags and additional chairs. Everywhere, we see armed guards standing at attention. Once we are in the hall, we are ushered to the head table and introduced to the top military commanders. Although we have been told they expect something useful from us, I'm not sure they are willing to trust a band of non-Arabs.

The hall is hushed as Arafat and his entourage enter. Arafat is flanked on both sides by two guards with machine guns. I notice that he seems shorter in person than on TV. Arafat has heard all about me and acts pleased to meet us. Dave monitors the satellite relay equipment. Gary keeps the camera running. Marsha holds her microphone near our faces. Marsha turns to Arafat and introduces herself and her team. He smiles politely and reminds her that for security purposes, after my speech she will be excused so they can discuss confidential issues. Arafat sits. Everyone else takes their seats. Arafat nods to Ambassador Haddam who then introduces me as an American mystic who should be heard.

I stand without knowing what I am going to say. I look at Jim, and he nods confidently. I stand before the microphone and have no thoughts. Several anxious seconds pass. I wonder if last night has erased my powers. I remember my out-of-body experience. I close my eyes and see Allah descending on a cloud. He stands before me and smiles like an old friend. I open my eyes and mouth, and at that moment, although the assembled group does not realize it, it is Allah who speaks in

Arabic through me. "My friends, why do you pretend to fight for a God in whom you do not believe? Mohammed—peace be upon him—says Allah is all powerful. If you really believed Allah is all powerful, you would not trust your guns. If Allah is all powerful, he will defend you from all harm. Your weapons testify to Allah that you do not believe his prophet, may he rest in peace. Why do you show Allah that you believe he is so weak that he needs your puny guns to defend his people?"

I am stunned. I am as surprised as anyone to hear these words from Allah through my mouth. The audience gasps as if a nonbeliever had abused their holy Koran, and a low rumble of anger is audible.

I hear Allah continue, while the crowd only hears a heretic abusing their faith. "You are hypocrites and liars. You pass laws to enforce the words of Allah. But does not his word say your only duty is public preaching? Your laws show that you do not believe Allah knows what he is talking about. You are telling Allah that you do not believe he is all knowing. You presume to tell Allah how to run his business. You say Allah is the only God, yet you put yourselves above him. What makes you believe you have a right to call yourselves the people of Allah? Turn to the true words of Allah. Believe he is all-powerful and throw away your arms. Believe he is all-knowing and repeal all your laws that enforce his sacraments. Let Allah deal with the nonbelievers. Let Allah deal with your enemies. Put yourselves in the hands of Allah and believe in him."

One of Arafat's generals stands sharply from his seat. I pause at the interruption. He marches around the table and stands before me. He is several inches taller than me and probably fifty pounds heavier. His heavy mustache adds to his imposing image. He is distraught. He shouts in Arabic, and I understand perfectly: "How dare you address us in this manner! You have been treated graciously. You are our guest. This impolite behavior is unacceptable. Apologize or die!"

"The truth is the truth," I respond.

"Do you believe Allah is all-powerful?"

"Yes," I proclaim.

"Do you believe Allah can protect you from my pistol?"

I see a .45 revolver six inches from my nose. "Yes."

"You expect us to believe that you trust Allah to defend you from my pistol?"

"You will believe as you will believe. Allah will do what he will. I have no reason to fear."

My vision is gone before I can see the explosion. My hearing is gone before the sound of the gun reaches my ears. The bullet enters my forehead and explodes out the back of my skull. It passes between Arafat and Haddam and lodges in the wall. It is surrounded by patches of blood and small chunks of my skull and hair. The president and ambassador are splattered with blood. My body collapses to the floor. The audience is stunned. The camera is rolling. Jim runs to my body and begins coaching me. Another shot rings out, and Jim falls dead on my corpse. The camera keeps rolling. Miss Clark recoils in fear as the pistol is turned on her.

"Stop!" shouts Arafat. "She is a famous American. She has value. She and her crew can help us communicate our demands. They are hostages. They are useful prisoners. Take them away."

Chapter XII

We're Dead, Jim

Well, here I am again. I see horizon all around. Above is solid white, and below is solid black. Looking around, I see a person walking toward me from the distance. I recognize that it's Jim. We speak alone in the whiteness.

"Well, Ken, so this is your famous out-of-body place?"

"Yeah, I guess so."

"How could you have given them the Jesus speech? That was really stupid of you."

"What do you mean, the Jesus speech?" I ask.

"You called them hypocrites and liars—hardly original. You challenged their honesty. Jesus did that to the Jews for the express purpose of getting himself crucified." His sarcastic tone indicates that he is angrier with me than I expected. "Truth-tellers throughout history have given that speech and been stoned, burned, crucified, or killed some terrible way. You must have suspected they would kill you. And now, I'm dead too, so I can't coach you back to life. If we still had our bodies, I just might kick your butt. How could you do this to us?"

"I let Allah speak," I say.

"Allah, Schmallah!" shouts Jim. "You know that is just a cop-out. You said yourself that all your gods are just figments of your imagination. Next, you'll be blaming your sins on the devil or some other demon. You know, Ken, you can't have freedom if you aren't willing to accept responsibility. I know you think Allah takes charge, but I'm sure you had the power to refuse to give that suicide speech. Search your soul—or what's left of it—and you will see that you could have told Allah how stupid it was. I guess you think you are some kind of medium or prophet. You know what I think? I think you are just an immature kid, unwilling to outgrow his imaginary friends. Now we're both dead, and I don't think anyone is going to save us. I hope you like hell, 'cause that's where the stupid go."

"But they are hypocrites and liars. The speech was true," I complain.

"True and stupid," blurts Jim. "Now I guess we'll be here forever. Damn you!"

Jim is the crabbiest dead guy I've ever met. Personally, I don't see the point in panicking, especially now that I've realized I'm still extant enough to be capable of panicking. "Why shouldn't I be faithful to the truth?"

"You should realize," says Jim, "that it is stupid to be faithful to some truths. Wouldn't you lie to save a loved one? You could have saved us both by omitting that truth. So with nothing else to do, let's talk about truth—truth and control. Can you name one government on the planet that is not run by hypocrites and liars? That's how human societies run. All societies are based on fraud, including religious societies."

"Why?" I ask, sincerely curious.

"Oh, come on, Ken. Don't be so naive. Human governments have to be dishonest. They all stand for principles nobody can live. So they lie. Even in our beloved homeland of America, every government official takes an oath to support the Constitution. Then they ignore it at every turn. It's just too high and mighty for anyone to support it. If they did support it, the people would never tolerate them in office. Humans want to be taken care of and told what to do. That's impossible without violating the constitutional oath of office. So, politicians play word games and tell terrible, impossible lies. The people pretend to believe the lies because they are afraid of freedom. Everyone knows the government can't take less and give more. Do the math. That's why you can't be a government official, Ken. You can do no harm, and governments can do only harm."

"What do you mean they can only do harm?" I ask. "I have run for office several times, and every time I intended to do good while in office."

"Ken, you're so stupid. The only way government can protect you is to do harm or threaten harm to your enemies. When was the last time you heard of a government soldier learning to forgive and love his enemy? The police have guns, clubs, and cuffs. Just what do they do that isn't harm?"

"Isn't it good to defend ourselves?"

"Maybe so, but it's only being done through violence. And all that government violence certainly isn't producing anything remotely resembling peace on Earth. How many Christians do you know who are asking government to turn the other cheek, as Christ taught? At least we atheists don't pretend to have principles we know we can't follow."

"That's outrageous, Jim. You must have taken that bullet in the brain." I am beginning to feel anger.

"Nevertheless, government may be necessary, but it is definitely a necessary evil," says Jim.

"And I suppose you never heard of all the good our government is doing with foreign aid and all the services they provide Americans," I counter.

"Oh, Ken, you have so much to learn. Japan gives us a good price on cars, and we complain of dumping. Don't you see that it's the same with foreign aid? Our government just buys politicians and hurts the local economy every time. You're too smart for me to explain it."

"Okay, I opposed foreign aid on moral grounds, not because it does harm. I can see how it might, but what about helping the poor in America?"

"Two things, Ken: first, you have to look at both sides of the equation. Government cannot give as much as it takes. For every dollar it gives out, more than a dollar is taken from the economy. The net effect is always harmful to the people. Second, giving money to the people usually hurts them. For example, let's say that government decides to subsidize a charity. The people see that it is subsidized and no longer feel any need to contribute. They are cheated out of the spiritual blessings they receive from giving. Then, the volunteer help falls so much that the net effect is less support to the charity than before the government got involved. Finally, the government wants to take over with excessive controls that stifle some charities completely out of business. Government help can be like a farmer who pulls up a plant to help it grow. He might lift it over his head, making the corn as high as an elephant's eye. But in his eagerness to raise the plant, he is likely to pull the roots out of the ground. Besides, no matter how high you hold a young sapling, in the case of many plants, you can never lift it as high as it would eventually grow without your help. The same principle applies when governments try to lift up the people. That's the usual result with individuals and organizations on welfare."

"Okay, I'm convinced," I say. "Governments can only do harm, and they should be prevented from trying to help. Let them limit their harm to criminals and enemies. But you didn't only condemn government. You said the leaders of every religion are guilty of hypocrisy and lies. I suppose you can explain that outrageous remark."

"Now I'm getting even angrier with you," says Jim. "You get me killed, and then you refuse to see the truth right before you. The problem with religious organizations is the same as government. Their beliefs are too high. They can't live their beliefs, so they invent long lists of trivial commandments. The members can live the trivial commandments. Doing so makes them feel good in spite of not being able to live the important ones. You can get in big trouble for violating a trivial rule, such as one that forbids the eating of pork, drinking a beer, eating meat on Friday, or having sex without government permission. But how many people have been chastised by their religious leaders for violating the important commandments, such as love your neighbors and tolerate them as you would like them to tolerate you? Love is the fundamental faith of virtually every religion and culture. Didn't Jesus put love at the top of his list? When was the last time your church excommunicated a member for asking government to violate the rights of others? Isn't it far more important to use government to prevent others from controlling freedom than to avoid tobacco and coffee? Don't you see the hypocrisy? Of course, your church is not alone. Every one of them is guilty of focusing on trivial rules while ignoring the really big stuff."

"You mean they strain at gnats and swallow camels?" I offer.

"There you go again, using Jesus's metaphors," Jim snaps.

"You know, Jim, you are right. For an atheist, you sure know a lot about Jesus."

"Yes, Ken, as I said before, I would bet the average atheist knows more about the beliefs and history of religion than the average believer. We have to, for self-defense."

"So what you're saying is—"

"What I'm saying is that every society is guilty of hypocrisy," says Jim. "It's part of the system. And if you wanted to make peace, you should have made peace. Reminding them of their big secret was a death wish. Surely there must have been a better way. Now, you've dragged me with you into this ... this God-awful place." He gestures around us, but I don't see what's so terrible about the place. I've certainly been to worse places; he clearly hasn't spent much time in budget motels.

"The last time I was here, after falling from a fire escape, I was told my conversation was only a figment of my imagination. Do you think maybe you and your words are just figments of my imagination?" I suggest.

"Of course they are, Ken. We are both just figments of your imagination."

"No, I mean, am I imagining that we are imaginary, or am I imagining we are real?" I say.

"How do we know the imagination imagining us isn't a figment of some other, higher imagination?" laughs Jim.

"And who is imagining that imagination?" I ask, perplexed.

"Well, Ken, I suspect the imagining goes in one great eternal circle. So, if you are anywhere on the circle, you are the ultimate imaginer and the ultimate imaginee at the same time."

"So, we imagine the imaginers who imagine us?" I suggest.

"Why not?" says Jim. What scientific evidence is there to favor our being imagined versus our doing the imagining?"

"If all is imaginary, how can there be such a thing as scientific evidence?" I ponder out loud.

"There is no evidence to support the idea that anything is real," says Jim, matter-of-factly.

"Well, Jim, do you suppose in the book of Genesis, where it says man was created in the image of God, it could have meant God created us in his imagination?"

"Or, Ken, maybe he imagined us in his creation—or maybe both. Aren't there two distinct creations in Genesis? Being an atheist doesn't mean I don't know your Bible. If it's so easy for you to imagine that man exists only in the imagination of God, why can't you just as easily imagine that God exists only in the imagination of man?"

"I can't imagine. So, are you are saying we are figments of our imagination's imaginary imaginer?"

"Something like that." Jim continues laughing at our conversation. "And Ken, it's okay to be plugged into the matrix as long as you are aware and in control."

"And how does one become aware and gain control?" I ask sincerely.

"There you go again with your 'how' questioning. If you are asking how, you are in your mind, and your mind can only know what it is told. There is another part of you that already knows. Didn't you learn anything from your healing?"

"So, if the all-knowing God is just a part of me, why can't I go there?" I ask.

"How do you know you can't?" challenges Jim.

"How do you know you can?" I challenge back.

"Now, you've gone too far for an atheist," laughs Jim.

"Doesn't your presence here prove your atheism is wrong?" I ask.

"No," says Jim sternly. "Atheists believe what they can see. I can see this experience, so I can believe it and still be an atheist."

"But Jim, do you remember my quote from the Koran on the airplane?"

"You mean that long boring one?"

"Yes. If you were listening, you would remember that Mohammed says it is too bad for those who don't believe until they see a sign. Also, do you remember the words of Jesus to Thomas that it is better to believe without seeing? Wouldn't you be better off to believe what you can't see?"

"Well, Ken, of course Jesus and Mohammed would say that, mainly because people don't exercise their spirituality without faith in the results. And if you don't understand the process, it's easier just to believe in an imaginary God who knows all and can do all. Nearly everyone has more spiritual power when they trust some all-knowing, all-powerful alter ego. It's like Dumbo's feather that enabled him to fly. I think there is a third category of spirituality even greater than those who believe without seeing, and I'm not talking about people like doubting Thomas who need a sign to believe. I'm talking about people who believe in themselves and exercise their spiritual powers without needing to know how and without needing some imaginary magician to do it for them."

"But what if you are wrong, and there really is a God out there?" I ask.

"If my atheism is wrong, I now challenge God to show His face and tell me I'm wrong," says Jim with confidence.

"According to my experience," I reply, "you see the God you expect."

"Fine," says Jim. "Then there will be no gods in this out-of-body experience. I rest my case." He crosses his arms in front of him, looking triumphant for the benefit of absolutely no one, since I've already learned not to feel too impressed by his debate-team antics.

"You know, Jim, it confuses the hell out of me that we are having this experience together. I mean, if each of us gets what we expect, and no two people expect exactly the same thing, then how can both of us get what we expect? In my first experience, I expected to see a roomful of gods and enjoyed every one. Now, I was hoping for more enlightenment. Why should my out-of-body experience be ruined by your lack of expectations?"

"Okay, look, Ken," says Jim, "the only way either of us is going to see anything is if we can agree on something we both expect."

"Or we could find some way to have this experience separately," I suggest desperately.

"Any ideas?" asks Jim.

"No," I reply. "Do you have any ideas why I only saw what I expected? Why can't the real God appear and teach us what to expect? I mean, how am I supposed to learn anything if I can only see what I already expect?"

"I think if you see something you don't already believe," says Jim, "that would force you to believe what you don't believe. I think that would violate the rule against forcing people's minds."

"Makes sense, I guess. But we're still stuck here, and my mission is a failure," I complain. I've come back from the dead once, so you would think I'd be an expert by now, but I have no idea how to get out of this place. If I can't go back to my efforts on earth, I would at least like to sign in to my golden villa or listen to some harp music or something.

"Let's try this," says Jim. "I accept the fact that you should have been killed by your fall when you were Santa. I accept the notion that you had an experience with some imaginary spirit. I also accept the notion that you were somehow able to think yourself back to life when you should have been dead. My records strongly support those conclusions, and they are conclusions an atheist cannot ignore. So, based on that premise, there must be a way for us to return to our bodies—without understanding how, of course."

"I agree. If we can get them back, will you forgive me?" I plead.

"I'm glad you value my forgiveness," says Jim. "Yes, damn it, I forgive you."

Suddenly, we hear a voice. Jim stiffens in surprise, but the voice sounds familiar to me; I've heard it before. "You have made peace. It is well. Both of you will return to life. You will experience no pain. Your bodies will be restored as if you had never been shot. It will happen when the time is right. You, Ken, must listen to Jim. He is wiser than you on many topics, and your success in establishing peace will depend on your willingness to accept his advice. You, Jim, must listen to Ken. He also has wisdom that you lack. Now you both understand why people must be allowed to be different. You need each other for completion. Working together, both of you will achieve your goals. Ken will build peace, and Jim will build his fortune. Watch now as events unfold, and the time for your resurrection approaches."

Chapter XIII

The Second Coming

Like many reports of near-death, Jim and I experience our invisible spirits hovering over our dead bodies. Obviously, our conversation in the spirit world did not take any time in the physical world. We watch from above as our bodies are placed on tables in the marketplace, like two sides of beef. The people mock and spit on our dead bodies. Tomorrow is Saturday, April 7. Sunday is the full moon and the beginning of Passover. Hovering near our bodies, we hear everything, including secret conversations and plans. We are surprised to hear that the Palestinian uprising is scheduled for Monday at sundown. They talk about needing three days to arrange the secret arrival of military gear from other Muslim countries. Iraq prepares missiles. Saudi Arabia prepares airplanes. Freedom fighters in Israel will disarm the Israeli nuclear missiles. Israel is scheduled for annihilation. A signal fire is planned on a mountaintop west of Jerusalem. Our bodies will be carried to the fire and consumed as the first enemy casualties. Miss Clark will televise the ceremony with a live satellite connection to the entire world. Then, the Muslim people will show the Jewish and Christian nations what can be done in the name of Allah!

We listen to this kind of talk for three and a half days after our bodies are placed on tables in the streets, and they stink. A crowd has gathered, but few are willing to approach within spitting distance. They have planned a procession to the mountaintop, led by our bodies on a trailer. The world watches through Marsha's eyes during the speeches that precede the march. My killer has become a folk hero. He speaks to an enthusiastic crowd.

"Al-hamdulillah! Ambassador Haddam has admitted he was tricked by this man's language skills. Allah did not say we should appear naked before our enemies. He said he would provide us with coats of mail to protect us from our enemies. He did not say that receiving his gift of shielding mail was a sign of disbelief. It would be an insult to Allah to reject the implements of war he has provided. It would be an insult to Allah to reject military assistance from our Muslim allies. Allah has blessed us with intelligence. It would be an insult to Allah to refuse to use our minds and stupidly expect Allah to wipe our hind parts with his right hand."

The crowd roars at the humor. The camera rolls. Someone screams. They point at my moving body. My head has completely reformed. I sit up on the table and look around. I turn to Jim, and he responds by sitting up. We slide off our tables and stand whole. The crowd is on its knees and faces. Arafat is stunned. My killer is terrified.

Ambassador Haddam shouts, "Stop the TV!" The three closest soldiers rush to stop Gary. Before they can reach him, he is floating five meters above the limestone pavement. Dave, the producer, is not so lucky. His equipment is immediately seized. Gary immediately turns his camera on Dave and his smashed satellite relay dish, knowing the camera includes a tape for future release.

I have a vision of Mr. Sands, back in Chicago. He watches in amazement as the picture and sound from his monitor suddenly become more clear and powerful. "Ladies and gentlemen," he announces to the world, "you are watching the demolition of our satellite uplink. As you can see and hear, the signal has improved. There is no mechanism known to science whereby the signal from that camera could extend more than a few hundred feet, much less reach our satellite."

From Chicago, the signal is relayed to network headquarters in New York and from there to the world. The whole world watches an event that cannot be, through a process that cannot be.

By the time I reach the microphone, I am live on virtually every TV and radio station on the planet. I face my killer, whose Adam's apple is bobbing up and down as he tries to swallow his fear of this strange, unstoppable man—a man he shot to death not long ago. His lips press tightly together under that familiar mustache—the one I saw right before he killed me.

I address him personally, in Arabic, although he seems more inclined to turn and run away screaming. "My friend, you have killed me. I forgive you. I would be honored to have you as a friend. Let us work together for peace."

His shoulders slump in relief and amazement, and he whispers "Al-hamdulillah."

The crowd whispers, "Al-hamdulillah."

I turn to the crowd. "To all of you who have abused and

mocked my body and the body of my friend, you are forgiven. Let us examine the lesson we are learning. When victims forgive, it gives them power. Do you not see how powerful the spirit of Allah is with me and my friend now? Do you not see the wisdom of Allah in letting this man kill us so we could show you the power of a forgiving victim? Your first step to freedom must be a complete forgiveness of your oppressors. That will put you in a position of power. They are watching tonight's events on their televisions. By tomorrow, the entire world will have seen these events. Now, we will make peace in Canaan. Tomorrow at sunrise, we will gather at this place. Everyone is invited, including the children.

"Each of us will carry a single stone in our fists. We will hold our stones high and march to the Al-Aksa Mosque, known as the Dome of the Rock on the Temple Mount. There, we will put our stones in a single pile as an offering of peace to the Jewish God, Ha-Shem—Jehovah. We will not surrender. We will never surrender. We will silence all the fears that motivate our Jewish oppressors. We will no longer use violence. We will make peace in peaceful ways. Ishmael is the father of all Arabs, and Isaac is the father of all Jews. Isaac and Ishmael were brothers. We will respect the descendants of our ancestor's brother. We will insist that they respect the descendants of their ancestor's brother. We will respect each individual's rights to choose his or her God, culture, and language. We will work together to pass laws that respect each individual's freedoms. We will resolve our territorial disputes as brothers, not as enemies. Jerusalem will finally live up to its name—house of peace—as it becomes the place where world peace begins." Some raise their arms in praise; others raise them in doubt. I insist, "They will not reject our offer. Their God will not allow it. I have met Ha-Shem and Allah, and they are one."

I hear a mix of cheers and boos. A few turn and walk away. I try to assure them. "The root of the issue is in the Dome of the Rock. Since before our era, the Jews have dreamed of rebuilding Solomon's temple. Then, a few hundred years after Jesus, the Muslims owned Jerusalem. They built this holy mosque on the site from which Mohammed rose to heaven. Unfortunately, it was also the site of Solomon's temple. Our objective will be to resolve this issue in a peaceful way. We will learn to respect each other and worship in peace. We will find a peaceful solution. It is finally time."

Chapter XIV

Stones for Peace

THE NEXT MORNING, IN our suite, I ponder our experience. I wonder if Jim, an atheist, can have spiritual experiences or how he would define them. I hope that somehow my good friend can feel the spirit. We walk in silence to the gathering site.

Few Palestinians have slept, as they spent the night preparing for the grand march. Practically every Muslim in Palestine has found a special stone to put on the Temple Rock. By the time the sun has fully arisen, there are dozens of television crews to record the march. Jim, Arafat, and I, along with my "killer," Anwar Ahmad, lead the procession. The Jews have seen my miracle. They have heard my speech. They have no choice but to allow the parade for peace. The entire procession route is lined with Israeli soldiers. It takes us over six hours to hike the ten miles, with the crowd graciously staying behind the fat man at the lead. In the early afternoon we begin placing our stones on the Temple Rock. By sunset, the pile of stones is higher than a streetlight. Throughout the night, more and more Muslims come and throw their stones on the pile. The next morning, the pile of stones is almost as huge as the Al-Aksa Mosque of the Dome of the Rock behind it. I have made arrangements to dress as an Orthodox Jew. A podium has been assembled with the pile of stones as a backdrop. The morning sun is peeking over the Al-Aksa Mosque, due east of our stones and podium. The enormous crowd makes room for the podium and photographers in front of the pile of stones. Again, I am invited to address the throng. Again, I have no idea what words will come from my mouth. I only know that my good friend Ha-Shem/Jehovah will speak in Hebrew through me. Without any introduction, I step aside and he speaks through me:

"This holy week, we celebrate the feast of the Passover. Moses achieved freedom for his people without a single violent act. He trusted Ha-Shem. Today, I ask all who believe in Ha-Shem to follow the example of Moses and trust Ha-Shem. Let Ha-Shem decide how to deal with unbelievers. Let Ha-Shem decide how He will run his society. Let Ha-Shem be your true God. Four thousand years ago, Isaac and Ishmael were brothers. The Muslims descend from Ishmael, and the Jews descend from Isaac. Yesterday, I told the descendants of Ishmael that they would obtain spiritual power through forgiving their oppressors. Today, I suggest the same tactic to you. Your ancestors have been oppressed almost continuously since before they walked through the Red Sea. Think of all your oppressors throughout history, from Pharaoh to the Philistines to the Assyrians to the Babylonians to the Nazis. Forgive them. In your hearts, ask Ha-Shem to forgive and bless them. Give them your mercy. Notice the spiritual power this gives you. Forgive all the sins of the children of Ishmael since they carried

Joseph into Egypt in slavery until the last stone was thrown just days ago. Let the children of brothers be brothers.

"As you prepare for the Passover feast, some of you will set an extra place for the prophet Elijah. Let us ask ourselves what Elijah would do if he were here today. Perhaps he would show the power of Ha-Shem, as he showed it to the priests of Baal. Perhaps he would ask Ha-Shem to accept an offering, a peace offering. Perhaps he would prepare a virgin red cow to be offered to Ha-Shem. Let the will of Ha-Shem be."

There is a commotion at the back of the crowd as a half-ton red heifer slowly walks directly into the crowd. Like a Texas Longhorn, her horns are six feet from tip to tip. The audience gives the heifer a wide berth, and everyone watches in silence as she strolls casually past the podium to the pile of stones. Carefully, she paws at the stones and then begins her ascent. She walks to the top of the pile without slipping. She sits down, faces the people, and begins chewing her cud. The crowd remains silent, and the whole world watches. The heifer coughs up an extra large bolus of cud, chokes, gasps, struggles, and collapses into death.

I watch with joy as I anticipate seeing a repeat of the Old Testament miracle of Elijah. I thank the gods. Then I shout into the microphones, "Please stay back! Let the will of Ha-Shem be!"

A cold wind blows across the crowd. I feel Elijah taking over as black clouds gather above. Suddenly, I see a young child approaching the pile to add his pebble. Before anyone can react, a bolt of lightning streaks down from the cloud and burns a black spot on the dead heifer's shoulders. The child is surprised but unharmed. His mother dashes from the crowd and carries him to safety. I am relieved. Then Elijah takes over again, repeating his Old Testament miracle of fire from heaven consuming a sacrificial red heifer. Another bolt of lightning hurls down on the heifer. Along the lightning bolt, a large ball of fire descends slowly. Little is known about this phenomenon called ball lightning, but it is apparently an eddy of charged particles swirling in a ball of light and electricity. Ball lightning rarely exceeds a few inches in diameter, but this ball of fire is a meter across. It explodes on the heifer and vaporizes her into a cloud of white smoke. I am suddenly reminded of the ritual in the book of Numbers, where a red heifer is cremated and her ashes purify the believers.

Another bolt of lightning brings with it an even larger ball of fire. This ball lightning transforms the entire pile of stones into a black pillar of smoke that lingers a moment before being blown away. A third ball, as big as the first two combined, crashes down on the temple rock, excavating a crater as deep as the stones had been high. The smoke clears. The clouds blow away. The crowd is silent for several seconds. Both Jews and Muslims believe in and celebrate having seen a repeat of a miracle from their ancient scriptures.

Chapter XV

The Wisdom of Solomon

"LET ME TELL YOU a story." The Spirit of Ha-Shem, or Jehovah, is speaking through me. The crowd is attentive and reverent.

"Solomon was a very wise man. He built a temple to his God on this place. He knew his temple would not stand forever. He also knew it would someday be rebuilt. Being very wise, he had his workers make duplicates of every temple utensil and ornament. At the bottom of the crater that was just created is a passageway to Solomon's secret vault. In it are all the gold, brass, and silver needed for the new temple. All other necessary items of temple furniture and all the plans and instructions are included. Also, we will discover the original Ark of the Covenant, built by Moses, in that vault. Solomon prepared us for this day."

No one speaks. Jim smiles. As I look around, I see open eyes and gaping jaws. How many times lately have I seen that same sight, that human sea of faces all nearly blank with wonder? Still, it never fails to move me. *This is really happening*, I remind myself. *The world is changing, right in front of me, right now.*

Ha-Shem continues speaking through me. "The great secret of the Masons was the fact that Solomon had an exact copy of the ark built. An even greater secret, one that died with a select few of Solomon's men, was the fact that more than one copy was made. In fact, three copies were constructed. All the workers believed they were working on the only copy. They thought they were keeping the ultimate secret, when, in fact, they had no knowledge of the other copies. The ark of Moses was carefully stashed with the duplicate temple treasures in the ultra-secret vault that has not been opened since Solomon sealed it, exactly three thousand years ago on the last day of Passover. Solomon believed that the power of the ark would serve his people, even if they did not see it. One copy was kept in the Holy of Holies, the most sacred room in the temple, for the annual high priests' ritual. One copy was sent to Solomon's friends in Ethiopia. They were instructed to return it when the temple was to be rebuilt. They thought they had the original and that a copy was in the temple. Those Jews who knew about the Ethiopian ark thought it was the only copy. They kept their secrets within secrets.

"There were three arks in and beneath the temple. One copy was in the Holy of Holies. One copy was in a vault, where the high priests knew of it. The original was in the vault beneath us, and nobody knew about it. Twenty-six hundred years ago, about a month before the Babylonians conquered Jerusalem, the prophet Jeremiah switched the arks. He believed he was leaving a copy in the Holy of Holies for the Babylonians to find and taking the original into hiding. Ultimately, he and one of the daughters of King Zedekiah ended up in what is now Ireland, where she married into royalty. Expecting to return eventually to Jerusalem, Jeremiah directed the building of a burial vault, containing what he thought was the original ark. It has been in Ireland all these centuries. Jeremiah is buried with it.

"When the conquering soldiers of Nebuchadnezzar found the ark in the Holy of Holies, they believed they had the source of Jewish spiritual power. If they had not found it, they might have killed and searched until all of Judah was eliminated. Nebuchadnezzar kept it in a place of honor as a sign of his dominion. When he began to fear for his kingdom, he built a hiding place in the great city of Babylon. He did not want an enemy to have this source of power or return it to the Jews. The three replica arks have spent all this time in Ethiopia, Ireland, and Babylon, while the original never left its holy place under the Temple Mount."

Now the crowd is excited. I feel the power of the moment.

"Hallelujah!" someone shouts.

"Hallelujah!" half the crowd answers.

"Al-hamdulillah!" someone else shouts.

"Al-hamdulillah!" the other half of the crowd responds.

"Hallelujah and al-hamdulillah!" another person shouts.

"Hallelujah and al-hamdulillah!" everyone shouts. I see Jews and Muslims shaking hands and hugging with new hope for peace. The spirit shows me the cheer echoing around the world.

Chapter XVI

Africans Bearing Gifts

AFTER SEVERAL MINUTES OF cheering, there is another commotion on the same street on which the red heifer had appeared. It's a small truck trying to get through. "Make way! Make way!" someone is shouting in Arabic. "We have the Ark of the Covenant!" It's the Ethiopians. Jim tells me their priests have seen yesterday's TV reports and believe it is time to fulfill their ancestors' covenant with Solomon. I ask how he knows.

"I know about the Ethiopians," says Jim, "for the same reason I am familiar with your Mormon history. The study of world religions has been my lifetime passion."

Respectfully, the Ethiopians take the ends of two carrying poles and bring their ark to the podium at the edge of the crater. The gold plating on the ark glistens in the noonday sun. Their three-thousand-year-old relic is in perfect condition.

"Please, use caution," I advise. "The ark was an electrical device, known in our day as a capacitor or condenser. The inner and outer layers of gold are separated by wood. The lid is in contact with the inner gold and not the outer. If it is charged, it can hold enough electrical power to kill a man. Before attempting to open it, you must use a wooden pole and a piece of metal to make the connection between the lid and the outer gold. That will discharge the electricity. Then, you can safely remove the lid."

"We have not opened it in all these three thousand years," says the head of the Ethiopian priests. "It was not ours to open. Here, look on the side, and you will see a plaque. It is Egyptian. It reads, 'Property of King Solomon.' Of course, the word is not Solomon or Shlomo—that was his Hebrew name. In order to please his non-Jewish subjects without offending his Jewish citizens, he took on the royal title, Son of Israel, King of the Canaanites. We believe you deserve that title."

I reach to the back of my neck and unhook the gold clasp on my dog tag. Happily, the Palestinians had not found it on my dead body—they never suspected I would be wearing such a thing, and my body was a bloody mess when they threw it on the table. I remove my dog tag now and hand it to the priest. He holds it next to the three-thousand-year-old plaque. The inscriptions are identical—hieroglyphs that spell my name as the son of Israel, king of the Canaanites. Marsha directs Gary, our cameraman, to get a close-up for the whole world to see. Two or three dozen other TV cameras close in for a shot. On the back side of my dog tag is the inscription "Sandra Anderson loves Ken Larsen."

The Ethiopian priest returns to the microphones. "You say you have come here to make peace. You have around your neck the royal title of Solomon. Did you know that the name Solomon means peacemaker?" The priest and I embrace, and the crowd cheers. "Hallelujah and al-hamdulillah! Al-hamdulillah and hallelujah!"

I sense the presence of Solomon's spirit. I open the ark, reach in, and take out and hold up a golden book. Solomon speaks in English for the world, pausing regularly for the Hebrew and Arabic translators. "If this ark is mine, then I have the right to give it to the people of Africa. Please, take this on behalf of your whole continent. This ark contains a copy of the Words of God, as revealed through Moses. They are inscribed in hieroglyphics, the international language of the time of Solomon, on tablets of gold. Let your scholars study them and publish them to the world. Then, if you are willing, I ask you to take this ark on a tour of all of Africa. Invite the spiritual leaders of every tribe, language, culture, and belief to add their records to the ark. Perhaps you will build another African ark to hold the overflow. Let all the beliefs of all the peoples of Africa be joined in one. Publish the records so that all can learn about all. Let all be considered worthy of respect. Ask the governments throughout your continent to enact the following law: 'Perfect toleration of religious sentiment is guaranteed. No inhabitant of or visitor to this state shall ever be molested, in person or property, by any person or by any agency or officer of any government on account of his or her mode of religious worship or personal pursuit of happiness, provided that such religious worship or personal pursuit of happiness shall not directly and physically harm or endanger the life, liberty, or property of an unwilling victim.' Teach tolerance everywhere you go. Teach employers and businessmen and landlords to respect the beliefs and lifestyles of others.

"Then, if you are willing, ask the governments of your

continent to form a commission of leaders from each religion and culture in all of Africa. Let this commission consider and rule on all international disputes. Resolve your disputes like the brothers that you are.

"To everyone in Africa who can hear my voice, I invite you to talk with your business leaders, your community leaders, your religious leaders, and your political leaders. Tell them how eager you are to work with them. Tell them how much you will love, honor, respect, and obey them as they work to enact this plan for peace throughout Africa.

"Finally, if you carry out my request, if all of Africa comes together in peace, I will ask the spirits to reveal the cures to all the diseases that now plague your lands. Those of sufficient faith will be cured immediately. The rest will respond to new medicines that are about to be revealed to science. Everyone who believes and touches this ark will be healed. Remember to touch the lid only."

A very poised older man with white hair, wearing a crisp suit, approaches the microphone without interference. Jim whispers, "It's the prime minister, Ariel Sharon." Concerned for his people, Sharon steps up and says, "Sir, these people are hungry and tired. Many of them have been here all night."

"You're absolutely right. Thank you," I reply. "Let's take the evening off and meet again tomorrow at sunrise. I doubt you'll have any security problems."

"I would be deeply honored," says the prime minister, "if you and your party would be my personal guests tonight."

"The honor is mine," I respond. "I suppose we will have a lot of things to discuss."

I turn to the crowd. "Brothers and sisters, we are going to

go to our separate places for food and rest. Please try to restrain your curiosity and stay out of the crater in the rock. You know that if your God has kept it secure for three thousand years, He will watch it one more night. Believe what your eyes have seen, and do not tempt your God. For those with insufficient faith, I must warn you on two points: First, the vault of Solomon remains sealed and will require several hours to open. Second, when Solomon sealed his vault, he left fires burning within. There is a poisonous atmosphere in the vault. The air in the vault has been free of oxygen for three thousand years. The first workers to open the vault will need breathing gear and ventilation equipment. If any of you do find your way into the vault, we will find your bodies later. Now, please return peacefully to your homes. Please tolerate each other. Help each other. Find your way safely to your homes. Tomorrow, at sunrise, we will have more visitors. I'll see you then."

Chapter XVII

Tolerant of Intolerance

Away from the microphones and shielded by security guards, Mr. Sharon asks, "How many will you be this evening?"

"There are seven of us," I reply.

"Wait a minute," says Jim. "There are only five in our party."

"You forgot to count my two Palestinian wives."

The prime minister looks at me curiously. "You have been in Israel only a few days, half of which you spent dead, and yet you have found not one wife but two? And just which God do you believe has approved of that?"

"A good way to develop tolerance is to exercise it," I reply. "I met two wonderful women five days ago. Despite having known each other for such a short time, we have enjoyed hours upon hours of conversation and laughter, not to mention ... well, we are incredibly compatible in every way. There's nothing impure about such consuming joy. It doesn't take long to recognize when another person exists on that same wavelength you thought you occupied by yourself. Even luckier, I've found two people, and how am I to choose? What divine indication has there been that I should have to? We immediately fell in love and decided we were married. I hope to raise children with them, in spite of my age. We are husband and wives. We are husband and wives because we say we are. If all legitimate governmental powers come from the consent of the governed, just where do individuals get the moral right to assign to government the authority to dictate the conditions of my marriage? Where do they get the right to demand that I ask their permission with a marriage license or a public ceremony? Would you respect me if I lived up to your standards or any other standards in which I do not believe, while violating my own? Wouldn't the world be better off if we allowed each man and woman to measure himself or herself morally against his or her own standards? Here is a chance for you to demonstrate your tolerance. Would you judge me and ignore the wives and concubines of Solomon? Didn't Solomon make peace by marrying the daughters of his enemies? What was the moral authority for Solomon's marriages? How about the marriage of Adam and Eve? Which government or church authorized it?"

Prime Minister Sharon pauses and then apologizes. "I am sorry for expressing disapproval. Please forgive me."

"Wait a minute," interjects Jim. "Ken, you are out of line here. Tolerance and approval are very different. This man is trying to tolerate you, and you demand that he approve of you. How do you expect to teach tolerance if you can't tolerate a little disapproval? Your so-called wives don't approve of my lifestyle. They don't even like me, and yet they tolerate me, and I tolerate them. You owe the prime minister a sincere apology."

"You are right, Jim. Prime Minister Sharon, I apologize. That was my ego talking. It assumes that just because the Spirit has spoken through me that somehow I can say anything, and the Spirit will vindicate it. I spoke inappropriately. You are right to tell me when you believe my actions are wrong. Tolerance does not require approval or even friendship. I humbly beg your forgiveness."

"I am astonished," says Sharon. "Although I doubt I will ever agree with your personal morals, I respect your right to them. You have impressed me very much. I think you just might be the most humble man I have ever met. I know I could never call fire from the heavens and then apologize like that on the same day. I am honored to know a man such as you."

"Thank you for accepting my apology. And you, Prime Minister Sharon, you are the bravest man I have met. I don't think I could witness balls of fire from heaven and then chastise the man who called them forth. That was an act of amazing bravery. You know, Prime Minister, I was afraid you might react to my fire show like Queen Jezebel did when she heard about Elijah doing the same thing. Do you remember? She challenged Elijah to kill her, or she would kill him within twenty-four hours. I was afraid we would be enemies."

"And I thought you would do to me what Elijah did to the priests of Baal," Sharon responds. "Do you remember? I feared you would kill me, my ministers, and all of parliament, the Knesset, just as Elijah killed the 450 priests of Baal. The people have declared you king of the Canaanites. The land of Israel is yours to take. You toy with me as if I had some choice in the matter. I have been in mortal fear for my life and the life of my government since yesterday, when I saw you rise from that table in the Palestinian marketplace. I appreciate your sparing of us, but I have resolved not to grant you any more than the Temple Mount."

As we step into the prime minister's limousine, Jim steps into the conversation. "Mr. Prime Minister, I think you might want to know something about my friend here. Actually, you are in no danger. He has some rules. If I understand them correctly, he cannot use his power to cause harm, to force human behavior, or to enrich himself or others. You need not feel intimidated. The same power that prevents you from hurting him prevents him from hurting you. Throughout history, humans have been peaceful because they respected each other's ability to cause injury. Now, we are in a new age, where you two can be respectful, knowing that neither of you can harm the other. Imagine a world where everyone lives by Ken's rules. And, Mr. Prime Minister, when you decide how to make peace, it will be your decision. He cannot use his powers over your personal mental freedom."

The entire flavor of our relationship suddenly becomes even better, as the prime minister realizes I am no threat to his or anyone else's personal freedoms. I notice a visible relaxation in his shoulders.

Chapter XVIII

A New Host

At the residence of Prime Minister Ariel Sharon we are shown to our rooms. It is almost as plush as the Palestinian headquarters. I step carefully on the beautiful carpets and enjoy the paintings on the walls and statues in the corners. My grandfather was the head of an art department, so I think I recognize quality and expense. There is an army of reporters outside, but our Marsha has the prime minister to herself. She is in heaven. Jim and I have separate rooms, and we spend a few minutes refreshing ourselves and preparing for dinner. It turns out that our meal is a hastily arranged state dinner, formal reception line and all. We are introduced to dozens of dignitaries; practically everyone in the government wants to meet us. The general tone of the evening is cordial and polite, but I think many of these people view peace as defeat. They are disappointed that I have taken from them an excuse to vanquish their enemies. When we finally sit down to eat, I end up seated next to the prime minister. As the servers begin our meal, Mr. Sharon stands to address his guests.

"I'm sure everyone here is just a bit confused and nervous. To calm some of your concerns, I think you should know a secret. This man may have the power of King Solomon, but he is harmless. He may call fire from heaven and inspire the whole world to follow him, but his powers are limited. He cannot cause harm. He cannot kill us, as Elijah killed the priests of Baal."

The hall erupts with sighs of relief and nervous laughter.

"Further, he has no power over our minds. He cannot hypnotize us and make us his puppets. He must deal with us as we deal with each other. Our negotiations for peace will be true negotiations. We have several serious situations to resolve. First, how will we deal with the Palestinians, now that they have sworn off violence? We cannot be the evil oppressors and survive in world opinion. I have already ordered all our police and soldiers not to initiate force. We will restrain ourselves as long as they restrain themselves.

"Next, we must resolve our border disputes. Input from King Solomon will be graciously considered, but we will make the decisions. Finally, I think everyone agrees it is time to construct our temple. We must find a way to remove Al-Aksa Mosque, the Dome of the Rock, without violating the peace. The Muslim world considers that mosque as the third most holy site in all of Islam. What will we do if tens of thousands of Muslims occupy the mosque and refuse to leave? Our number one duty will be to look like the good guys. We must find a solution that will keep us looking honorable. I think we have made a good start. Right now, I am receiving reports of complete peace in the land as everyone awaits the outcome of tomorrow.

"Please think seriously on these issues. After the meal, my

administrators, military advisors, and leaders from the Knesset
will meet in my office for some preliminary discussions. Let's
plan on meeting one hour from now. Now please, enjoy your
meal."

The food is surprisingly good. I usually don't like lamb, but
this rack of lamb is perfect. Jim and I share a bit of laughter
as we learn how to eat ripe figs with knife and fork. After the
meal, we return briefly to our quarters. My wives graciously
remain in my room as the members of our media team remain
in theirs. A translator is arranged for Jim. After preliminary
introductions and opening remarks by the prime minister, I
am offered a chance to address the group. According to our
agreement, I ask if Jim can speak for me, as Aaron spoke for
Moses. The ministers are politely amused. Jim has some ideas.

"My friend, Dr. Ken Larsen, known as Solomon, or son
of Israel, king of the Canaanites, cannot be overlooked. The
people expect him to run the show tomorrow. For decades,
most Jews have dreamed of building the Temple of Solomon
on the Temple Mount. Now, they expect King Solomon II to
direct the construction of the temple. You cannot dismiss him
from this scene. May I suggest that he is capable of getting
you off the hook? You have a major public relations problem
here. You lay one hand on that Muslim mosque, and the entire
Muslim world will consider it an act of war. I suggest you deal
with this problem the way Pilate dealt with Jesus—wash your
hands of it. Let Ken here take all the heat. He has the title, and
the people have obviously accepted him. Give him the Temple
Mount. Deed it to him. Make it like the Vatican City in Rome.
Then he will have all the public relations problems with the
Muslim world. If anything goes wrong, the world will blame

Ken, and you will look very good as you take back your gift. If things go well, you will look good for having given it to Ken. This is a win/win. Give the Temple Mount to King Solomon here with the proviso that you will take it back if he fails to please everyone."

"That's brilliant!" exclaims an advisor.

"Pure genius!" echoes another.

"I so move!" rejoins a third.

"Wait a minute," interrupts another. "How can we deed Israeli land to a non-Jew? Besides violating our laws, won't this create some major public embarrassment?"

"What is your answer, King Solomon?" asks Prime Minister Sharon.

"I was raised a Mormon," I respond. "According to Mormon traditions, I am a descendant of Ephraim, son of Joseph, son of Israel. I am not of the tribe of Judah, but I am of Israel. Is it not true that Mormons who wish to immigrate to Israel are received with all the citizenship privileges of Jews?"

"Yes, that is true, but are you really a Mormon?" asks Sharon. "The last I heard, Mormons do not allow polygamy, especially your style."

"Actually, Mr. Prime Minister, I was excommunicated several years ago by the Mormons for having sex with a girlfriend." To be fair, the Mormons consider all kinds of things to be promiscuous; I hadn't even started my polygamy stage back then. "Would you deny citizenship to a Jew who had been excommunicated by one of your Orthodox sects for violating their traditions? Do you have a test of personal worthiness for immigrants? I believe my last name is evidence that my ancestors considered themselves of Israel. I think you can recognize that and avoid violating any of your laws or traditions."

Relieved, the prime minister counts unanimous hands. "Now we can work to resolve our differences with the Palestinians without the Temple Mount being part of the equation. This is good. King Solomon, tell us how much land you think you need."

"Actually," I respond, "I have been thinking about it. Are you willing to grant me, as King Solomon's successor, a circle of land one kilometer in diameter centered on the crater?"

"That is about the size of the ancient city. We will deed to you everything within the walled city. It won't be exactly circular, but it will exceed your space request. We will call it the land of Canaan, and it will be the limit of your kingdom. You will have no authority outside your kingdom. We will make your deed subject to a provision that we can repossess your kingdom at our pleasure. Thus, we will rescue it from you if you screw up, and we will be spared your problems with the Muslims. We will also require that you use the land only for temple-building. I think we are in sufficient accord that my secretary can prepare the proper documents and a release for the media tomorrow. Good, very good. I'm sure we can count on the Knesset to approve."

The Knesset leaders nod. Sharon continues. "Now, our good friend Solomon has suggested to the nations of Africa that they pass laws like the American Constitution and First Amendment." The cheering is unanimous. Sharon speaks again. "But since the days of Zedekiah, 2,600 years ago, our people have been persecuted virtually everywhere on the planet. Finally, we have a place of refuge where Jews are in charge. If we pass these laws, how will we prevent the return of the Palestinian refugees? How will we prevent the influx of Muslims until they have a majority and elect a Muslim government? I might be willing to tolerate the beliefs of others, but I'm not sure I'm willing to put our people at risk of becoming what they have been—a people without a homeland."

"Being tolerant does not mean being stupid," says one adviser.

"How will we protect our people from hatred?" asks another. The same sentiment is visibly expressed by other advisors.

"We have always been a religious country. Why can't we tolerate the religions of others without having them take over our lands?" says a third advisor.

"If we open our borders and grant citizenship to non-Jews, we cease to exist," a fourth complains.

A fifth advisor suggests, "Surely there must be another option."

A sixth gives his opinion, "How many Muslim countries treat Jews as second-class citizens? Huh? Too many. I say we agree to make Israel free for Muslims the same day the last Muslim country becomes free for Jews."

Everyone starts to murmur at once, exchanging anxious glances.

Jim raises his hand, and they fall silent. He clears his throat and his mind, preparing a response for them all. "Thank you for listening to me again. I think there is a way you can have it both ways. Suppose a Muslim entered Israel, and there was no land he could buy? Suppose all the land was privately owned by Jews who agreed not to sell their land to non-Jews for ... oh, let's say thirty years? The government would not be banning Muslims.

It would be respecting the property rights of private Jewish citizens to sell to whom they wish. What if all unoccupied land in Israel were divided up and deeded to private citizens? You could auction it to Jews only. In fact, just as you deed the land of Canaan to Solomon, you could deed all your unoccupied lands to anybody, maybe one of yourselves. Then, as a private property owner, he could auction it only to fellow Jews who agree not to sell it to non-Jews. There would be no place for non-Jewish immigrants. They would fill the houses now owned by Muslims. They would fill the hotels and inns now owned by Muslims. There would not be room for enough of them to become a majority. They would come to Israel and, just like Mary and Joseph, they would find no room at the Inn."

A few chuckles respond to the joke.

Jim continues. "All government-controlled lands could be deeded to one man or a small group. Then, as more and more Jews immigrate, settlements for them could be arranged by a private landlord. The government would not be discriminating, and you would not have any laws preventing private property owners from discriminating. Everyone would be free—free not to sell or rent to whomever they chose not to." Jim becomes more animated. "Then what would happen? The whole world will want to visit the land of Canaan. They will need a place to stay. They will need food and supplies and entertainment. They will bring their money. Some will sell their furniture to pay their way to visit the Temple of Solomon. You will line the west coast and the Dead Sea with resorts and hotels. Every square meter in all of Israel will be dedicated to serving your visitors and collecting personal fortunes. Shuttle busses will fill your streets. Tourists and pilgrims will fill your restaurants.

Your Muslim neighbors will busy themselves, providing food for your visitors. You will have the money to build dozens of desalination plants along both the Mediterranean and Red Seas. You will become the richest land in this part of the world, and you will do it without a single oil well. Every Jew in the world will want to be part of your bonanza. You will hardly have room for them all. The Muslims will be no threat. You will be too busy and wealthy to worry about a few Palestinian refugees trying to crowd into their limited space. Besides, why should they live in their brother's stable, like Mary and Joseph, when they can build mansions in other countries on the profits from selling you the food and other supplies that your visitors require? And why should they want to become the majority culture in Israel when your constitution forbids them from enforcing their beliefs? What are you going to do when every hotel chain in the world comes with their bags of money and requests the privilege of building a billion-dollar hotel on land they are willing to rent from one of you? This man has opened a treasure for Israel, and I'm not talking about the treasures of three thousand years ago."

The room is silent for almost a minute. Jim's message is as powerful as fire from the sky. Again, his proposal is accepted unanimously. Jim speaks. "Why don't you copy the United States of America? Become a national government with a national constitution and several states. Make Canaan a state. Make Palestine a state. Maybe make two or three other states. You are the national government. Your Supreme Court is the final court of appeals from within any state. When the American Constitution was ratified, with freedom of religion at the national level, some states required that public officers take a Christian oath. Later, they evolved; now, every state has freedom of religion. Why can't Israel take that intermediate step? Why not let each state within the nation of Israel resolve that issue? Let the Palestinians decide how they will deal with religious freedom in Palestine. Only require that they have a republican form of government in which leaders are chosen by the people and are constitutionally limited in their powers. Then, you don't have to deal with the Palestinians at all, as long as they respect the rights of their citizens. Civil laws can differ from state to state, within your constitutional limits. I think if you begin with that premise, it will be relatively easy to negotiate the drawing of the lines on your map. What do you think, Solomon?"

"What do you call it when an atheist is inspired?" I ask.

The group chuckles. Obviously, Jim has solved all three questions.

* * *

We are now in our rooms in the Palestinian headquarters. I place a return phone call to Utah, realizing that my hands are shaking as I press the buttons. Even after everything I've been through, I realize I am more afraid of hurting my family than I was of facing crowds in a strange land, disagreeing with extremely powerful men, or being shot in the head.

"Hello?"

I immediately recognize my oldest daughter's voice.

"Hi, honey," I manage through my emotion.

There is a pause—one of the longest pauses of my life. And then she explains that the entire family has been together at her house, trying to contact me for several hours. "We're all here, Daddy," she says gently. *Daddy.* She hasn't called me that in a long time, and I can almost see that little girl again, tucked under her covers. She interrupts my memories. "We're on speakerphone so we can meet as a family. First of all, we want you to know that we understand, and we forgive you. It's obvious why you had to do what you did." She seems to need to stop for a second to collect herself; then she says, "We're proud of you. Now come home already, will you?"

The tears I had hoped to hold back fall, but they have become tears of joy, and my family and I weep together.

After the intense but happy call, I report all the good news to my wives. Cheerfully, they reward me for my success.

At that point, it occurs to me to hope that my children like their new stepmothers. But something tells me it will be fine. Amazingly enough, Yin and Yang are not the strangest thing to have happened to my family lately!

Chapter XIX

Is Hate a Crime?

Stepping outside, I notice the nearly full moon on the western horizon. It fades in the glow of the dawn's early light. I think to myself that if Francis Scott Key were here, he could write another poem to liberty, maybe another national anthem.

The three-mile drive from the minister's mansion to Old Jerusalem is bumper to bumper. Jim and I ride with Prime Minister Sharon in his limousine. I wave through the open window at the cheering crowds.

Sharon turns to Jim. "You are an excellent political adviser. If ever you need a job, you have one with me."

Jim smiles and nods. "Actually, Mr. Sharon, I doubt I will ever need another job. Last night I was on the phone with my publisher."

"Really?" I ask.

"Yes. Actually, he called me. He made a few preliminary calls, and he already has advance orders for over ten million copies of our book. That number is probably several times as much by now. The book will wholesale for twenty dollars and retail for thirty. Three dollars from each book will go to the authors, one each for myself, Mr. Solomon over there, and Marsha Clark. I talked with Marsha, and she wants to divide half her royalties between Gary Clayton and Dave Brown. As soon as Ken agrees, my publishers will deposit thirty million dollars in our account—ten for me, ten for Ken, five for Marsha, and two and a half million each for Gary and Dave. I expect our annual royalties to be even greater for several years."

"Wow!" exclaims Sharon. "They have that much money?"

"Well, they will soon have two hundred million just for the advance orders up to now," replies Jim. "When Dave heard the good news, he said he had often watched Air Jordan playing for the Chicago Bulls and wished he could make that kind of money. Now, he will. Fortunately, the early chapters documenting Ken's recovery were mostly written before we left the States. I wrote two versions, one for the medical community and another for the man on the street. With illustrations from Marsha's videos, it should make a beautiful book. We are planning at least two editions, one before and the other after the temple of Solomon is complete. In the first edition, we will feature a drawing of Solomon's temple on the cover. The second edition will feature a photograph. No, Mr. Prime Minister, I don't think I will ever need another job. You are sitting with a couple of very rich authors. Heh-heh. How about it, Ken? Do you approve? This is not personal gain from your powers. It is just good business."

"Do as you will. I'm sure I can think of a good way to use the money," I respond, thinking of my children. I still feel that I owe them for putting them through so much sadness. Besides, I figure when one is balking at the idea of two new stepmothers, a few new houses will probably make the news much more palatable.

"Before we reach the Temple Mount," says Sharon, "I'd very much appreciate some free advice from a wealthy friend. I've been thinking about your idea that government should tolerate intolerance on the part of individuals. I believe I understand and agree that individuals must be free to choose their own way. I will support the complete elimination of government control of religion and personal lifestyles. I will not force individuals to act righteously or even act kindly to their neighbors. But of course, you expect me to prevent them from harming others?"

"Of course," Jim says, nodding.

"Well, I've been considering the following situation. Suppose an Arab attacks a Jew, or a Jew attacks an Arab. In this case, two crimes have been committed—first, the attack on the individual; and second, the attack on the culture. What do you think of the idea that the penalty should be more severe, maybe even double, if the victim is a member of a group that is obviously hated by the attacker?"

"We have a lot of laws like that in America," says Jim. "They're called laws against hate crimes, increasing the punishment of criminals for their words and presumed thoughts. I'm not in support of such laws. Let me explain, with an example. Suppose you are in grammar school at the age of nine or ten. At that age, young boys work out their relationships with their peers. Sometimes, as they develop their pecking order, so to speak, there is violence. Usually, before the violence, there are hateful and hurtful epithets hurled. Now, let's suppose in your classroom all the boys are Jewish, except for one Christian from Germany and one Muslim from Iraq. Further, let's suppose one of your Jewish classmates is a bully. He ends up hitting every other boy in the class, including you. Before each fight, he shouts obscene insults. He calls one boy stupid, another fat, and another skinny. He calls you a goy. He calls the Christian a Nazi and the Muslim a hashshash."

Sharon smiles at being called a non-Jew.

"Finally," Jim continues, "the aggressor is apprehended by the teacher. All the truth is known. The teacher announces that his punishment will be to apologize. He must apologize verbally and in writing to each of his victims. In addition, he must give them the equivalent of one hour's earnings—let's say about five dollars in American currency. That should stop the beatings. Then, suppose further that the teacher announces that the villain must give a stronger apology to the Christian and Muslim because he hated them for being goyim. Also, he is required to give them each ten dollars. Remember, you are only nine years old, the intellectual level at which most humans make lifetime social decisions. Put yourself in that situation, and imagine how you now feel toward your Christian and Muslim classmates."

Sharon appears deep in contemplation as Jim poses his questions.

"Are you glad the Muslim and Christian got twice as much as you got for being Jewish? Have you not been discriminated against? Do you love and admire these minority classmates more? Or do you resent them for getting a bigger reward for being hated? Are you going to be more likely or less likely to invite them to join your next game of football? If there is an argument over the rules, you will have to be more careful when yelling at or fighting with these privileged boys. Seeing that,

I predict you will not want them in your game. I predict you will be less motivated to invite them to your party, unless you fear that not inviting them will be seen as a hate crime. Your relationship with them will not be unrestrained. You will feel awkward and uncomfortable around them. You will be afraid to push them playfully. In fact, you will be motivated to avoid them. The result of the enforcement of this hate-crime law will be more hate, not less."

A Muslim woman pushes against the window and blows a kiss to Sharon. He is touched by the gesture and exclaims, "Love comes from the heart, not the law."

Jim is pleased. He makes his point. "The founders of America were very wise. They said that all men are created equal. Laws against hate crimes create special classes of people, just like affirmative action. They make some people more equal than others. People might be less likely to insult or attack them in ways that are illegal, but they will be more likely to discriminate against them in ways that are legal. You cannot preach equality by establishing inequality. In fact, I believe it is a hate crime to legislate against hate crimes. No, Mr. Prime Minister, I think Jews should be punished equally for attacking Muslims and Christians, as they are for attacking Jews."

"Thank you," says Sharon, smiling and waving at the cheering crowds. "I'll think about your advice."

Chapter XX

Ark! Ark!

Except for the mosque and a few important archeological sites, the Temple Mount is mostly rocks and gravel. Today, it is completely covered by people. Parking is impossible, and Sharon asks our driver to let us out, return to Sharon's home, and wait for a phone call to come and pick us up. Still, we have to walk about a kilometer to the Temple Mount and Al-Aksa Mosque, the Dome of the Rock. Sharon graciously requests permission to enter my kingdom. We laugh together. As we walk along, we hear religious songs of every style and language. We hear another message being shouted along the route, "The Iraqis are here! The Iraqis are here!" As we approach the mount, we see the cause of the commotion. Next to the podium is another ark, glistening in the early sunrise. Although identical in appearance, it is not the ark we saw yesterday. This one is surrounded by Iraqis. The crowds part as we approach the podium. I get a friendly wave from Marsha and her crew, who came early to set up. Although nearly everyone in Israel wants to be part of our crowd, the security personnel have restricted the first hundred yards to the media. We hear that every flight into Israel has been packed with media for the past day and night. I see cameras inscribed in languages I have never seen. I guess this is bigger than the Super Bowl.

When the cheering stops, Sharon speaks. "People of Israel. People of Palestine. People of the world. I have an announcement. Last night, I agreed to propose to the Knesset that Israel deed the entire ancient walled city to the son of Israel, king of the Canaanites. I believe the Knesset will agree. Please understand that we did not feel threatened or under any pressure to make this decision. We think it is a wise decision. Do you agree?"

"Hallelujah and al-hamdulillah!" the crowd cheers in deafening unison.

"Thank you. This will be the extent of King Solomon's kingdom. He will have no authority over the government of Israel. He will have limited authority over the Old City. If he abuses his position, we will reserve the right to repossess it. Now, I believe we have some guests who desire to be heard."

The ambassador from Iraq steps to the microphones. "Thank you, Prime Minister Sharon. Thank you, Lord King Solomon. Greetings, people of Palestine. Greetings, people of Israel. Greetings, people of the world. We are exhausted by our preparations and travels, but we wanted to be here to greet you this morning. Like the morning sunrise over the Dome of the Rock behind us, we bring light from the east. It was unknown to the entire world that a true replica of the Ark of the Covenant was hiding in our country, all these twenty-five and a half centuries. What the king of the Canaanites has said is exactly true. Nebuchadnezzar hid this ark when he feared the rising strength of his enemies to the south, centuries ago.

Just last October, the ruins of the ancient city of Babylon were jolted by an earthquake. An ancient vault was uncovered by the quake. Within it, government explorers found this ark. Immediately, it became top secret and was taken to Baghdad, where President Saddam Hussein hoped to use it as a bargaining tool for peace. When he saw yesterday's events, he decided to join the Palestinians in their quest for peace. With the return of this relic to its home, the people of Iraq ask for peace between our nations. We ask for an end to all economic and military sanctions against our people. We ask that all foreign military forces, including airplanes, immediately respect our sovereignty and our national airspace. We ask to trade freely with our brothers and sisters throughout the world. We ask that Muslims and Jews be treated fairly in all countries, including Arab countries and the homeland of our Palestinian brothers. In the name of Nebuchadnezzar, we apologize. We offer mutual forgiveness and extend the hand of peace."

The crowd erupts with delight as I embrace the Iraqi ambassador. Even greater applause is heard when Sharon steps forward and embraces the Iraqi. Carefully, I open the ark and withdraw a golden copy of the words of Moses. I step to the microphone to accept my gift. I speak in my own English, as translators relay my words in Arabic and Hebrew.

"Thank you. Let us all respect and appreciate the courage of President Hussein in returning this sacred relic when he could have used it as a tool of revenge. Let us do what we must to respect and answer his wise counsel for mutual forgiveness. We have a new millennium. Let us forgive the past. Let all nations try to forgive the past and begin anew as brothers. Just as I gave yesterday's copy of the ark to the continent of Africa,

I now give this copy to the entire continent of Asia. I ask you, Ambassador, to take this sacred relic to your president, Saddam Hussein. Ask him to please accept it on behalf of Asia. When I say Asia, I include Turkey, the Arabian and Indian peninsulas, and all the land eastward to the Pacific, including the islands of the sea and the subcontinent of Australia. As with Africa, I ask that a commission of Iraqi holy men take charge of this ark and negotiate a tour of all the lands of Asia. Let every culture add their holy writings to its contents. Let it be an instrument for peace among the Sunnis, the Shiites and all others who revere the Holy Koran. Let it bring peace between the Muslims of Pakistan and the Hindus of India."

What happens next, before I can finish my remarks, astounds even me.

Chapter XXI

A Slip of Tongues

I PAUSE FOR THE translators and hear nothing. Rather than staring expectantly at the translators, the crowd is cheering. The Hebrew translator is silent. The Arabic translator is silent. I look at the translators, and they shrug their shoulders. Jim, who is standing nearby, steps over and quietly says, "Like Pentecost, I think everyone hears you in his own language." I realize the Jews, the Muslims, and now the Christians have each seen a repeat of one of their famous miracles.

"Well, this is a pleasant surprise," I say. I go on to ask for peace between Buddhists and Communists in China, between Muslims and Christians in Indonesia, and everywhere that cultures clash. Then, I repeat my request that the governments of all these lands pass the same laws of tolerance I had recommended to Africa and establish an international commission of spiritual leaders to resolve international conflicts. I am about to finish my remarks when Solomon takes over, speaking through me. "Brothers and sisters of the world, it is time to commence a new age in human history. It is time to reset our minds as well as our calendars. We can set all scores at zero, not only cultural and national scores but individual scores as well. Let us work to eliminate the punishment of humans. I invite every prisoner in the world to open his or her heart to the Spirit. If they do, a spiritual counselor will appear to them exactly as they expect it. This counselor will provide them with the necessary therapy to heal them of their criminal inclinations. If their problems are medical or mental, they will be healed. New medicines will be revealed to cure those who are hopelessly addicted to narcotics and other dangerous drugs. When they are restored to civil health, another spirit will inform their superiors that they are ready for freedom. When they are free, their first mission will be to seek out their victims and repay them as much as they can. Perhaps they will simply work in the garden for their victims' families. I invite all victims to graciously accept these efforts and replace revenge and justice with forgiveness and mercy."

The crowd is silent. I turn to embrace every member of the Iraqi delegation. Reverently, they load their ark into the back of a small truck. Another commotion is heard from the crowd.

"It's the Irish! It's the Irish!" I hear from the crowd. Soon, the third and final copy of the Ark of the Covenant arrives at the podium. It turns out that the Irish caretaker of the tomb had a dream and felt compelled to exhume the vault where the ark was hidden. When our story hit the news, the authorities of Ireland immediately arranged shipment of their ark. Although their ark was not stolen, they felt compelled to fulfill the will of Jeremiah and bring their ark to Jerusalem for the temple. I ask them to take it back to Ireland and use it to patch up the conflicts between Protestant and Catholic Christians. I dedicate their ark to the healing of Europe and the Western Hemisphere.

Then, Solomon has a third special blessing. Just as the healing of disease in Africa and the healing of criminality in Asia apply to the entire world, this gift also is for the entire world. It has to do with the ball lightning that consumed the heifer and stones. Solomon continues speaking through me:

"It is with extreme pleasure that I announce the gift of peace given in the name of Europe and the Americas. You will call it a ball-lightning generator. You saw the tremendous energy in those balls of fire that came from the sky. There is a way to extract electricity from ball lightning. Your technicians will be inspired to learn how to configure a chamber so that charged particles or ions can be injected into a powerful magnetic field and will flow in a spiral. The spiral will move in a circle and close on itself. The magnetic forces generated by the spiral flow of ions will oscillate or vibrate in such a way as to absorb energy from the flowing ions. That magnetic energy will be harnessed by a sphere of wires, or transformer, surrounding the ball lightning. The power will flow along wires and drive your industry. Once you develop the machinery, you will be able to produce a one megawatt generator about two cubic meters in size, or the size of a common chest freezer, as cheaply as you now produce a small automobile."

Audible gasps are heard from the audience, and they murmur among themselves for a moment before Solomon continues. "The generator will require the addition of fuel, which can be any substance with polarity; that is, a plus and a minus side to each molecule. Water will do fine. As the energy is extracted, according to Einstein's formula, a single glass of water should be more than adequate to supply all the electrical needs for an average subdivision for a century or so. Jim, my advisor, has advised me not to use special powers to create wealth. But this will not be magic. Everything will be discovered and developed according to the laws of physics. Does anyone really believe inventions of the past were not revealed through spiritual powers? I sincerely apologize to those who now hold their wealth in oil and oil reserves. I encourage you quickly to invest your fortunes in ball-lightning generator development, manufacturing, and marketing."

The Iraqi diplomats listen intently, as Solomon paints a picture of worldwide prosperity.

"With this invention and the virtually unlimited cheap energy it will provide, the open spaces of the planet will become immediately habitable. With this energy you will be able to recycle everything. You will recycle your waste water through distillation. With abundant energy, your trash will economically provide new glass, plastics, and metals. Smoke from your industries will provide valuable chemicals as they are rendered pure. You will be able to extract glass and aluminum from common dirt. Glass and aluminum will replace wood as building materials. The ground you excavate for a building will provide most of the materials needed for construction. You will not need to destroy the world's natural forests. You will not need to pollute the air with the exhaust from your fossil fuels. The ball-lightning generator will have no exhaust. A single home, equipped with such a generator, will have no need for sewers, water lines, electric or gas power connections, or, with satellite communication, even telephone lines. You will be able to build and live comfortably in almost any place on the planet. Your trucks, trains, and ships will run endlessly without burning fossil fuels. Your cars and airplanes will burn hydrogen, made from water at little or no cost. Their exhaust will be clean water vapor. And as this generator will be easily portable, it will provide abundant energy to the most remote village."

The audience is so enraptured by the vision that they fall completely silent, transformed by wonder into human statues. Solomon shares more wisdom and counsel.

"I give only one warning. The space on this planet is limited. There is much value in preserving open spaces for wild plants and animals. While we enjoy the prosperity and comfort provided by cheap and plentiful energy, we must learn eventually to control our birthrate. Before we completely cover the globe to the exclusion of all wild creatures, before we run out of space and return to war, disease, and famine to limit our numbers, let us learn peaceful ways to live within the limits of our planet. While there is still room for growth, we have time to counsel together and mutually agree on voluntary ways to limit our reproductive expansion. Let all good men realize they cannot love their neighbors if they are adding to this problem. The condition for this gift is simple: stop fighting and find a peaceful way to preserve nature."

Chapter XXII

My Coronation

ANOTHER COMMOTION ANNOUNCES THE arrival of more visitors. This time, it's Queen Elizabeth of England with her royal entourage. The queen is dressed in her finest royal regalia, her crown glittering in tandem with her jewelry. The dozen or so members of her entourage are similarly dressed up for a royal celebration. The archbishop's robes touch the ground as he marches with his assistants. Behind them is a trailer with a large chest full of jewels and gold. The queen is not bringing an Ark of the Covenant, but her assistants are struggling with their large chest. She asks to speak. "King Solomon, England desires to be the first country to recognize your government. To help finance your kingdom, more than half the crown jewels of England are in this chest. Please, use them as you will. Now, I have a story for you. According to our traditions, when Jeremiah went to Ireland, he had the sacred sandstone block on which King David was crowned. It was the Foundation Stone, also called Jacob's Pillow. All the kings of Judah down to Zedekiah were crowned while sitting on this stone."

A golden sandstone cube, about a meter on a side and obviously matching the stones in the temple wall, is brought forward and placed before the podium. The queen continues:

"A few rulers of Ireland sat upon this stone to receive their crowns. Later, the stone was taken to Scotland and used for the crowning of their kings. The stone was captured and taken to London, where my ancestors received their crowns while seated upon it. It was under my coronation throne. Recently, we have returned the Foundation Stone to the people of Scotland as its rightful owners. Yesterday, the Scottish government contacted me, the last monarch to be crowned on Jacob's Pillow, and asked if I would bring it to you. This sandstone cube and the authority of the crown of King David belong to you. If you will kindly sit upon the stone, I have invited the archbishop of Westminster Abbey to bless you and transmit from me to you all the original authority of King David. I recognize you as the rightful heir to the throne of Solomon I and his father, King David."

As I step forward to sit on the sandstone, Jim whispers in my ear, "Your ego, Ken. Watch your ego." I smile in gratitude for the counsel and sit upon the rock. The crowd is hushed as the archbishop blesses me with the powers of the throne of David. Much to my surprise, an ancient English crown is taken from the treasure chest and placed on my head. A large purple robe is placed on my shoulders. Suddenly, I realize the value of Jim's advice. I struggle a moment to keep my ego from telling me I am somehow responsible for all this glory. I feel myself crying. I have difficulty hearing as the queen leads the crowd in a cheer.

"Long live King Solomon II. Long live the son of Israel, king of the Canaanites." The cheer is shouted several times. It is followed by shouts of "Hallelujah!" and "Al-hamdulillah!"

Queen Elizabeth suggests I find a proper office in which to receive diplomats. Sharon says Israel will provide. Sharon faces the queen and, speaking into the microphone, says, "In the name of Israel, I challenge England's claim to be the first to recognize King Solomon II. You were, however, a very close second," he chides in a friendly manner. The queen and prime minister shake hands and laugh together. "Now," announces Sharon, "we have three short days to prepare the feast of the Passover, and one of them is a Sabbath. Perhaps our host, King Solomon II, will allow us to set up an open-air feast here in Old Jerusalem." He looks at me and I nod. "And perhaps King Solomon II will allow me to make all the arrangements." Again he looks and again I nod. "We have much to organize," he says. "I hereby invite the leaders of all the countries of the world to come and celebrate with us. Our Passover feast will be Sunday, April 8, the same day as the Christian Easter. Let us celebrate this year as the brothers we are. I want Saddam Hussein to sit at my side. I want the leaders of the Muslim world to sit at my table. I want to invite all the leaders of nations now in strife with their neighbors to come and sit together at our feast. I hope you all enjoy rack of lamb. However, we will prepare to respect the wishes of our vegetarian brothers."

The crowd is peaceful. They have been together long enough to show obvious signs of fatigue. Again, I send them to their homes. "That concludes our gathering. Tomorrow, we will begin the project of opening the treasure vault at the bottom of the crater. I strongly recommend that you stay home and watch on your television sets so that you will see the vault and view the treasures as it is opened. We will bring forth the treasures and store them in a museum you can visit. Please, go home now. Thank you."

Chapter XXIII

An Intimate Dinner

I<small>T TAKES ALMOST AN</small> hour to finish shaking hands and hugging. It is heartwarming to see Sharon's enthusiasm as he embraces the ambassador from Iraq and Yasser Arafat. Jim suggests to Sharon that he invite Arafat to his home for a quiet evening meal together. The invitation is given and accepted. Sharon's limousine driver carefully takes us through the crowded streets to Sharon's residence.

As I wave at the crowds from my right-rear seat, Jim speaks from my left. "Ken, I hope you don't mind that Prime Minister Sharon and I have arranged a quiet meal tonight with Yasser Arafat."

I turn from the window and look at Jim. "Yes," I say, "that's a great idea." Sharon turns from his front seat and reaches back to shake hands with Jim and me. He motions for Arafat, who has been standing nearby, to join us. The limousine has plenty of room for three of us on the backseat.

"I have another idea," says Jim. "You both have been so

receptive to my ideas, I hope you don't mind one more." We nod for him to proceed. "Well," says Jim, "I know Ken is thinking about his plans for the Temple Mount and Old Jerusalem. I think Ken is capable of getting a vision to guide him. In fact, I think Ken is capable of sharing his vision with you, Prime Minister Sharon, and you, President Arafat."

Nothing can surprise me anymore, and that realization prompts me to reflect on how much my life has changed. It's hard to believe that just a short time ago, I was just a mall Santa, telling a little boy stories about world peace.

Jim and I look at each other in anticipation. Then, Jim explains himself. "Human traditions tell of many examples where a particularly powerful spiritual person has shown visions to others. I think Ken has that power. I think he can ask the Spirit to show him its plans and show them at the same time to others. Look, he has called fire from the sky. He has spoken and been understood in many languages. He has healed himself and others. He has given the gifts of physical and mental health. He has even promised cheap power to the entire world. I think this stunt is well within the range of his powers. How about it, Ken? Are you willing to try to share a vision concerning your temples?"

"Sure, why not? I'll try."

"Good. If you, Prime Minister Sharon, and you, President Arafat, can see the building of the temples, you might be able to discuss and approve them together. Then, you can assure your people and calm their fears. I know the Israelis fear the domination of the Arabs with their mosque of the Dome of the Rock. I also know the Muslims fear the removal of their sacred mosque. If you two can see eye to eye on the subject, peace will be advanced. I think Ken's power can show you a solution that will satisfy everyone."

"Now you have touched on the heart of the problem," says Sharon. "Since we became a nation in 1948 and won our independence in 1949, our people have planned the rebuilding of the Temple of Solomon. Nobody has thought of a way to build the temple without starting a terrible war. Obviously, the Al-Aksa Mosque must come down. But equally obvious is the fact that the Arab world will never allow it. There is not room on the Temple Mount for all the Muslims who will come and stand in our way. There must be ten million Muslims right now who are willing to die rather than let us destroy their sacred sanctuary. On the other hand, there are probably equally as many Israelis willing to give their lives to assure the building of our new temple. If you think the Spirit has a plan that will satisfy us both, I will be more impressed than I have been so far, fire balls and all. You do assure me that our feelings and decisions will be our own, correct? Ken will not use his powers to change our minds for us?

"I don't think he can," says Jim.

"I certainly don't want to," I add.

A pleasant dinner is completed and the four of us—Jim, Sharon, Arafat, and I—enter a small private room. Jim suggests we all sit comfortably on easy chairs. Sharon whispers to an assistant, and four easy chairs are arranged in a private room. I lean back on my chair and pull up the foot rest. I tell Sharon and Arafat that I met Jim immediately after getting my powers. They lean forward, showing interest. Briefly, I describe our meeting and my healing. I tell them that Jim was an atheist faith healer. They smile politely at my attempt to ease the stress of our situation. I suggest that we turn our attention to Jim.

Jim begins his coaching. "Prime Minister Sharon, do you believe the Torah?"

"Yes."

"Do you believe in Michael the archangel?

"Yes."

"Do you believe angels still have the power to speak to men and show them the future?"

"Yes."

"Do you believe Michael the archangel has the power to visit us and speak to you in Hebrew?"

"Yes."

"Good. President Arafat, do you believe the Koran?"

"Yes, of course."

"Do you believe the words in the Koran, which say that the angel Gabriel caused the Koran to descend on the heart of Mohammed by the permission of God?"

"Yes. You know of that?"

"I have been doing some research. Do you believe that Michael, the archangel of Allah, could speak to Prime Minister Sharon in Hebrew and have the power to speak to you in Arabic at the same time?"

"Yes."

"Good. Ken, are you willing to allow Michael the archangel to speak to you in English while these men hear him and converse with him in their own languages?"

"Yes."

"I think you are ready. Do any of you mind if I join your vision?"

"No."

"No."

"No."

Chapter XXIV

Better Than TV

THE FOUR OF US lean back in our chairs and face the wall behind the desk. I notice a hint of fear and suspicion in the eyes of Sharon and Arafat. Their pursed lips suggest a determination not to see their people betrayed. I suspect they are not yet comfortable with the idea that there can be a winner without a loser. They stare at the wall as the action begins. A light appears in the center of the wall and grows until it is about three yards in diameter. A figure in a white robe appears in the light. He stands in the air a dozen centimeters above the top of the desk. The four of us are stunned simultaneously. "Fear not," he says, smiling and opening his arms in greeting. "I am Michael, the archangel of your creator. I am the chief of all angels. The angels under my supervision and I have spoken to many Hebrew prophets, as well as to the Muslim prophet Mohammed. We also have spoken to several Christian prophets and prophetesses, including Mary, the mother of Jesus. My message for all of you is the same: love each other. As I describe the future for the Temple Mount, you will see scenes on the wall at my right. If you have any questions, do not hesitate to ask."

Obviously, each of us hears and understands comfortably. Michael begins the show, and we share a vision of the future.

"Tomorrow, you will open Solomon's vault and put his treasures in a museum. Then, you will organize for the work to be done. Thousands of workers will be hired and paid an American salary—twenty dollars an hour. Each team of workers for the preliminary stages will have two supervisors, one Jew and one Muslim. They will agree before giving a directive. You two, Sharon and Arafat, will oversee the organization of the workers. Solomon II will provide funds with the sale of some of his English jewels. He will also give some of his book money for the construction effort. Soon, there will be plenty of money from around the world and plenty of skilled workers to do the work."

On the wall, we see tens of thousands of happy workers. It's not the same as TV or a movie; it looks like a window into three-dimensional reality.

Michael continues. "After the safe removal of Solomon's treasures, you will survey a circle of one kilometer in diameter, centered on the crater. Every structure within the circle will be removed, except the Muslim mosque. Each statue, shrine, and edifice will be carefully removed and restored outside the circle. You will remove and rebuild, just as your Egyptian brothers removed and rebuilt their ancient structures in the path of Aswan waters. When all the holy and archeological sites have been fully excavated and removed, you will build the holy mountain. You will go to the slopes on the western shores of the Dead Sea and quarry the limestone for the holy mountain. You will build up the north, west, and south slopes of the mountain until all is perfectly level within a circle with a radius of one-half kilometer. Stairs and elevators will facilitate the ascent of visitors to the round table. This will be the preliminary work. Thus, all structures on the holy mountain will be equal in height and grandeur with the mosque. Then, you will survey and mark two inner circles, with the crater as their center. One will have a radius of one-quarter kilometer and the other, one-eighth kilometer."

I notice that Jim is busy taking notes as the diagram appears before us.

"The outer ring, one-quarter kilometer wide, will be divided into eight equal portions, corresponding to the cardinal directions and their diagonals. The Eastern portion will remain the Muslim mosque of the Dome of the Rock. Next to it, in the northeast portion, will be the temple of Solomon. In the north will be a Christian cathedral. Northwest will be a Buddhist shrine. West will be a temple to pagans and all other spiritual groups not specified. Southwest will be a temple of Taoism. South will be Hindu. Southeast will be a shrine to atheism, agnosticism and science. Finally, in the center, you will build the Eye of Horus."

We see eight magnificent temples on a level mountain, equal in stature and grandeur, surrounding an Egyptian pyramid. Sharon is the first to admit it. "It never occurred to me that there might be room for all of us on that mountain, much less that our places of worship might fit so beautifully together." The rest of us nod and smile.

Michael continues. "Each Muslim sect with more than a million members will designate one person to form a board of governors for the mosque. All Muslim sects with fewer than a million members may unite and send one delegate. That board will have final say, and all their decisions will be unanimous. They will be responsible for maintenance and scheduling. They will receive the entire world and share their doctrines without animosity."

Arafat is smiling broadly. New scenes appear as the narration continues.

"Those who work to build the Temple of Solomon will be required to prove that they are Jews and that their parents and grandparents were Jews. A board of directors will be chosen, with one member from each Jewish sect with a million members or more, as with the Muslims. After the sacred relics and Ark of the Covenant have been placed in the temple and blessed, only Kohen, the true inheritors of the Jewish clergy, will touch them."

Sharon is smiling from ear to ear. We watch, spellbound, as seven more magnificent structures rise before our eyes.

"The Christian, Buddhist, pagan, Taoist, and Hindu temples and shrines will be built in a similar manner, under the direction of boards of directors, with one member from each sect with over a million members. Never mind that some directors will be delegated from churches having ten or a hundred times as many members as others. It is the various doctrines, not the memberships, that must have equal footing. All decisions will be unanimous. I will avail myself to those who ask."

Arafat has a question. "You mean anyone on any board of directors will be able to ask for and receive a vision from you at any time?"

"Yes," says Michael.

Sharon grins and asks, "You won't need an apartment, will you?"

"No. I will appear only as requested."

Both Sharon and Arafat continue smiling as the archangel continues.

"The temple to atheism and agnosticism will be an observatory, planetarium, and museum of science and technology. The universities of the world will contribute leadership and resources for its construction."

"What about the Eye of Horus?" I ask.

"The Eye of Horus, in the center over the crater, will be built under the supervision of the Baha'i faith. I will now describe it for you as you see it on the wall behind me. Within the one-fourth kilometer diameter circle, they will build an octagon ten meters high. Each side will face one of the eight temples. The sides will bear the following colors: east, red; northeast, blue; north, white; northwest, orange; west, black; southwest, green; south, yellow; southeast, indigo. Each side will have a separate entrance. Above each entrance will be one of the trigrams of the I Ching, as follows: east, second son; northeast, father; north, first son; northwest, third daughter; west, second daughter; southwest, mother; south, first daughter; and southeast, third son. Above the octagon, they will build a pyramid with four sides on its base. The ratio of the height of the pyramid to a side of its base will be 2 over pi, exactly as with the pyramids of Egypt."

As Michael speaks, we see a giant building behind him. It is about six hundred feet, or two football fields, wide. The octagon is about three stories high. Each of the eight sides is a different color and covered with the inscriptions and symbols of the temple it faces. The three bars of the I Ching are above each entrance. Each of the three horizontal bars is thirty feet long and three feet high and covered with gold. The pyramid above the octagon is about a third as high as the Empire State Building. We are amazed at its impressive size.

Michael continues. "Near the top, on the north side, will be an entrance to a shaft down the center of the pyramid. The inside of the pyramid will be a hollow spherical gallery, one hundred meters across and covered with polished gold, forming a mirror. There will be a concourse around the sphere, just within the outer walls. Doors from the outside will be offset from the eight doors into the central gallery, so that light from the outer doors cannot pass through. In the center of the gallery, they will establish a crystal sphere, twenty meters in diameter. It will be supported on the backs of twelve golden oxen. Around the sphere they will build sloped seating, as in a coliseum. A mirror will be mounted at the top of the shaft to receive sunlight and reflect it below to the crystal sphere. Another mirror will be built on a tower fifty meters high, immediately south of the Christian cathedral. It will be parabolic and computer-controlled to constantly reflect the rays of the sun onto the mirror at the top of the pyramid. Thus, the rays of the sun will illuminate the crystal sphere inside the pyramid. Ken will write a book about his experiences, and I will inspire him to prepare a drawing of a cross-section of the pyramid for the front cover. The eight outer temples are for meeting and instruction. The Eye of Horus will be for silent meditation only. Visitors will wrap their shoes in cloth for soundproofing. There will be no speaking or other communication among visitors. Each visitor will silently enter and sit before the crystal sphere until he or she is satisfied. Then he or she will depart in silence."

"How will they build such a crystal ball?" I ask.

"A giant spherical mold of clay will be heated to the melting point of crystal. It will be erected on the spot before the construction of the pyramid. When sufficient sand has been added, the crystal will remain molten for six months to allow all the air bubbles to rise to the top. Then, it will be gradually cooled, over a period of two years to prevent cracking. Finally, it will be gently polished until it is perfectly round and smooth. Then, it will be draped with canvas as the pyramid is built around and above it. Further instructions will be given as needed."

"Wow!" I exclaim.

The archangel speaks. "Every belief and culture on your planet will have a holy place on this site. Admittance through the outer walls will require only that the entrant repeat convincingly, 'I am willing to be touched by the light to accept all humans as my own brothers and sisters.' Once within the walls, everyone will hear the speech of all others in his or her own language."

Sharon and Arafat turn to survey each other with obvious emotion, as if each man is seeing the other for the first time.

Michael continues. "Those with conflicts to settle will come together in this place. After a few moments of silent meditation before the Eye of Horus, they will worship in whichever house of worship suits them. Then, they will gather in some outside meeting place to resolve their conflict. Political treaties, labor-management disputes, family quarrels, and all kinds of human conflict will find peaceful resolution because of this place.

Jerusalem will fulfill its destiny and become a true house of peace."

Jim appears very satisfied with himself.

"Are there any questions?" asks the archangel.

Sharon and Arafat look at each other several seconds.

Sharon speaks. "It's a miracle. I have seen the answer to our national dilemma. I believe this will satisfy everyone, including all Jews and Muslims. What do you think, Mr. Arafat?"

Although Sharon speaks in Hebrew, Arafat hears in Arabic.

"I agree completely," says an astonished Arafat with eyes wide open. His speech is strained from breathless realization. "You have found a way to build the Temple of Solomon without offending a single Muslim. Since our edifice is already completed, I will suggest to my people that they assist all the others. We can provide building materials. We can quarry the rocks. We can feed and clothe the workers. I'm sure many of our people will want to work on the observatory."

"And your workers will not receive a penny less than any others," says Sharon.

"I suspect most of them will happily donate most or all of their pay to the holy cause," retorts Arafat.

Chapter XXV

The Future

I RAISE MY HAND to pose my only question. "I suppose I will have a role in all this construction, but I'm not sure what it will be. What am I expected to do during and after the construction? It looks like every square foot of the holy mount will be directed by others."

"Yes, Ken," says Michael, "your work here is almost done. Soon, you will receive requests from others. Wealthy men will see the advantage of having a holy mount and a New Jerusalem. You will oversee a worldwide franchise system. Replicas of the holy mount and all its temples will be built in Ethiopia, Iraq, and Ireland to house their copies of the Ark of the Covenant. You will build additional copies, and they will have the powers of the originals. You will build holy mounts in North and South America, in India, China, and Australia. As Jim has pointed out, men will become rich as visitors stay in their hotels, dine in their restaurants, and enjoy their resorts. The Mormons will help you build a New Jerusalem in the center of the United States of America, where their founder has already laid the foundation stones for their great temple in Jackson County, Missouri. In every holy mount, men will understand each other and feel inspired to love and tolerate. According to your traditions, at the time of the Tower of Babel, the language of men was confused, so they could not communicate. Since then, humans have diversified and lost the ability to see eye to eye. Now, as they look into the Eye of Horus, they will see eye to eye. The confusion of languages is over."

I look at Jim, who is grinning and nodding with enthusiasm. "Jim," I say with a smile, "I think your atheism is slipping."

"I have a secret," says Jim. "I'm not an atheist. Neither am I a homosexual. I lied about being a homosexual so that I would be able to avoid sexual encounters. I cannot have sex. I am what you might call a nondenominational angel."

I am stunned. All this time, my closest and most trusted friend was fooling me about being homosexual and mortal. Part of me feels betrayed. Another part of me is overwhelmed at the idea of working with a true angel who is willing to spend so much time and energy to help me. I also realize I could not have worked so closely with Jim as a friend and an equal if I had known. Now, I watch in awe as two angels work for me. When I asked for the wisdom of Solomon, it never occurred to me to ask for angel assistants. I'm glad somebody thought of it. I take Jim's hand and realize I argued with an angel. What could he have done to me? I feel extreme gratitude and love.

"Well, Jim," says Michael. "Are you coming?"

Jim shakes my hand, hugs me warmly, and whispers in my ear, "Remember, Ken, never trust a man who claims he cannot lie. That claim is always a lie. Be sure to check my notes for completeness, before you forget anything." Jim walks over to Michael the archangel. "How did I do, Mike?" he asks.

"You did pretty well, Brother Jim," responds the archangel, "but you didn't have to be so hard on those missionaries."

"Oh, they'll get over it," says Jim. "You know they will be stronger once they get their spiritual confirmations again. Besides, I'm not the first angel to play around with the clergy."

"Come along, Jim," says the archangel. "We'll discuss this more on the other side."

The light grows again. Jim and Mike walk into the light. It fades, and they are gone.

I step over to Jim's chair and pick up his notepad. It reads: "I, Dr. James Nephi Teasdale, do hereby bequeath all my personal papers, records, and manuscripts to my good friend, Dr. Kenneth Rex Larsen. I also bequeath to him my share of the royalties on our book, which is now his book."

As I write these words, I think about my adventure. Everything is pretty well automatic, as temple mounts multiply. I have two beautiful wives who love me. I have all the wealth and popularity I ever could have dreamed of. My eight children, their spouses, and my twelve grandchildren love me, my wives, and their new homes. Life is good.

And the conclusion? All the governments, cultures, languages, races, and religions have agreed to peace and tolerance. I wonder how long the peace on Earth will last.

Regardless of how long humanity can maintain this moment, we are happy for now.

Credits

Peace on Earth—An Answer

Featuring, in order of appearance:

Ken Larsen, the author, known as King Solomon II, or son of Israel, king of the Canaanites, who, in his efforts to demonstrate tolerance, gives equal time to the metric and English measuring systems

Martha, the little girl who believes in Santa

Billy Mitchell, the rascal with the recorder, who, as an adult, will make a perfect Santa

Mr. Burton, who gave Santa's paycheck to his wife

Sandra Anderson, whose next boyfriend introduces her to marijuana, so the adulteress in this story will be stoned

Jed Anderson, the jealous husband who will never stop trying to find a way to sue Ken

The Spirit, who appeared to Ken as a thousand gods

Suzy the nurse, who always suspected Teasdale wasn't exactly human

Dr. James N. Teasdale, nondenominational angel, translated being, third Nephite

Dr. Jones, the neurosurgeon who never said a word

Marsha Clark, who will own her own TV station

Mr. Sands, who will own a national network

Gary Clayton, the multimillionaire cameraman

David Brown, the multimillionaire producer whose mansion will be next to Gary's

Elder Smith, who will be president of the Jerusalem Mission

Elder Young, who will be president of the Palestine Mission

The unseen flight attendant for Air France, who brags to her friends about her famous passengers

The Muslim who sold Ken his clothes and now displays Ken's as holy relics

Ambassador Haddam, who tells his grandchildren he never really doubted Ken

The two Israelis, who heard the Koran in Hebrew and didn't know how to report it

Yin and Yang, Ken's two Palestinian wives, who will give him many more delights, including three children

Yasser Arafat, who still needs a shave

Anwar Ahmad, the impetuous general who killed Ken and still brags about it

The Ethiopian priests, who will run their own holy mountain

Ariel Sharon, prime minister of Israel, minus Old Jerusalem

Sharon's advisers, yes-men, every one

Ken's children, who were heard and not seen

The Iraqi ambassador, who somehow never had a name

The translators who stopped translating

The Irish, whose ark actually contained the bones of a leprechaun

Queen Elizabeth, who hugs quite well for an older woman

The archbishop of Westminster, who pinched my ear during his blessing

Michael the archangel, a figment of Sharon's, Arafat's, Jim's, and Ken's imaginations

And finally, the crowds, mobs, police, and soldiers, without whom this story would have been less exciting

Happy Christmas to all, and to all a good night!

Postscript

In case you want to know what the two angels said on the other side ...

As Jim and the archangel reach the other side, Jim says, "I'm sorry I was so rough on those two Mormon missionaries. Ken needed to hear what I had to say. I realize I dumped some spiritual knowledge on Elders Smith and Young for which they weren't ready."

Michael says, "I was serious about this. Since Smith and Young saw your King Solomon do his stunt, they have been deeply concerned. For several days, both of them have been intensely involved in personal study and prayer. I have some plans for them. I think it's time to give each of them a vision. Tonight, you will visit Elder Young, and tomorrow you will appear to Elder Smith. You will tell them about your experiences as a Nephite apostle. You will restore their spiritual confidence."

"Sure, Boss, no problem," says Jim. "I'll hold their hands while they move up to a higher level."

"Excellent," says Michael.

"You know, Mike," says Jim, "I think he still hasn't figured out who he is."

"You mean Ken?" says the archangel. "I think you're right. Do you think we should tell him?"

"No, not at all," says Jim. "He's doing perfectly. Besides, I'm not sure his ego is ready. Give him time. He's got a thousand years."

"Very well," says Michael, "But do try to help him understand in plenty of time to prepare for his final battle."

"Sure, no problem. I'm kinda going to miss the good old days before peace on Earth."

"Yeah, me too."

"We've come a long way together, and now it's almost over."

"Indeed, indeed."

With arms over each other's shoulders, the two angels walk off into the nothingness.

Afterword

HAVING COMPLETED THE STORY, I'm not so sure peace is a good idea. Maybe peace is too boring. Several of my reviewers complained that this story about peace is too peaceful. If we need conflict and opposition in something as trivial as this bedtime story, maybe we're not ready for peace on Earth. Well, anyway, I hope you enjoyed reading as much as I enjoyed writing. Thank you.

About the Author

My qualifications include a PhD in Zoology, an intense lifelong interest in mysticism and my involvement of fourty years in politics. I was born and raised in Provo, Utah. As a devout Mormon, I became an expert in the scriptures and the principles of our Founders (inspired by God, according to Mormonism). At a young age I decided my life's goal would be to become such an expert in science and religion that I could resolve their differences. Hence, I was a Mormon Missionary in France, where I was exposed to many religions and cultures. My PhD is about the evolution of a group of lizards. I failed in my life's goal to unite science and religion. Then, I discovered the relationship between the teachings of religion and the principles of the Founders. America is about love: treating others as you would have them treat you. My book is about the mystical path to peace on earth.

I now live in Salt Lake City with my love, Rebecca, and her son, Gabe. Being retired, I spend much of my time at the local Senior Center, playing harmonica, singing with a choir, and acting in plays. Three of my five children live in Salt Lake County with their children. Another lives in Tooele, Utah, and the youngest is in Los Angelos building an acting career.

My book, *Peace On Earth*, is a fantasy experience in which I tell my own biography, along with my dreams and aspirations.